CW00665096

Praise for OUR SHADOWS

Shortlisted for the 2021 Victorian Premier's Literary Award for Fiction • Shortlisted for the 2021 Voss Literary Prize • Shortlisted for the 2021 ARA Historical Novel Prize

'When lists are made of the great novels of the Australian landscape, [*Our Shadows*] deserves to be among them.' *AUSTRALIAN*

'A masterwork.' *RN BOOKSHELF*

'Written like the wave that haunts its imaginative landscape, ebbing and flowing from past generations to the present and back again.' *GUARDIAN*

'Another virtuoso performance...Poetic and beautifully crafted.' *AUSTRALIAN BOOK REVIEW*

Praise for THE DEATH OF NOAH GLASS

Winner of the 2019 Prime Minister's Literary Award for Fiction • Winner of the 2020 Literature Fiction Award in the Adelaide Festival Awards • Shortlisted for the 2019 Miles Franklin Literary Award • Shortlisted for the 2019 Victorian Premier's Literary Award for Fiction • Shortlisted for the 2019 ALS Gold Medal • Shortlisted for the 2019 Voss Literary Prize • Shortlisted for the 2019 Colin Roderick Award

'Swooningly lyrical, carrying the reader along in the wake of its beauty.' *AUSTRALIAN BOOK REVIEW*

'*The Death of Noah Glass* is among [Jones's] finest work and I expect it will be among this year's outstanding novels.' *AUSTRALIAN*

'As always it is the links and echoes, the patterns that [Jones] sees in life and the way such patterns are represented and become part of our internal landscape that inform and fascinate, and make her work so rewarding.' *ADELAIDE ADVERTISER*

'[A] polished, pensive novel that swirls so much about, tantalising with implications amid the patterned intricacy of linked scenes, returning symbols and motifs.' *SATURDAY PAPER*

'Another rich and accomplished work.' *SYDNEY MORNING HERALD*

ALSO BY GAIL JONES

GAIL JONES

SALONIKA BURNING

TEXT PUBLISHING MELBOURNE AUSTRALIA

The Text Publishing Company acknowledges the Traditional Owners of the country on which we work, the Wurundjeri people of the Kulin Nation, and pays respect to their Elders past and present.

textpublishing.com.au

The Text Publishing Company
Wurundjeri Country, Level 6, Royal Bank Chambers, 287 Collins Street, Melbourne Victoria 3000 Australia

The Text Publishing Company (UK) Ltd
130 Wood Street, London EC2V 6DL, United Kingdom

Published by The Text Publishing Company, 2022

Jacket design by W. H. Chong
Jacket images by iStock
Page design by Rachel Aitken
Typeset in Granjon LT Std 12.5 /18pt by J&M Typesetting

Printed and bound in Australia by Griffin Press, an accredited ISO/NZS 14001:2004 Environmental Management System printer.

ISBN: 9781922458834 (paperback)
ISBN: 9781922791108 (ebook)

A catalogue record for this book is available from the National Library of Australia.

The house, our hair, everything close
and dear, even the air,

is burning! In our hands
(we had no warning
of this) the world is alive and dangerous.

David Malouf, 'Ladybird', *Earth Hour* (2014)

BY MIDNIGHT ALL was blaze and disintegration.

A group of soldiers standing on the hill watched with indecent pleasure. The wind locals called the Vardaris blasted from the north, puffed minarets into candles and monuments to blocks of gold. A whoosh of flame—shaped paisley in its exotic unfurling—caused some spontaneously, shamelessly, to exclaim and clap.

No one would have said it aloud: *How strangely beautiful, a city burning.*

But alarm, infant fear, the sufferings of others: these were no match for excitement at a safe distance and the view of roaring engulfment, the way flame hurtled at the sky, reached for new fuel, burst light on the polished marble of churches, synagogues and mosques. The markets were gone, and the luxury stores on Eleftherias Square. The French Quarter was destroyed, the Café Cristal, the Hotel Olympia, the town hall, the Athens Bank. The English post office on Frangon Street was a pile of hot rubble.

Among the first to burn were the Ottoman houses in the old town. Wooden balconies fell into laneways in splintering crashes; rooms held shape until the last second, in nests of amber light. Smoke and ash, detachment, they all made up the show. There was a villainous cracking sound, like the smash of a headstone with an axe, then sparks and black arising in thick, gusty blurts. *Whoomph*, another gone; and the sound entering your bones.

Look! A cat falling, its fur on fire, poor thing. Or was it a shred of something solid, moved by distortions of flame-light? The soldiers could not see a confirming detail, but the story was a good one, a doomed cat leaping or flung, burning in a ball as it fell.

Such a hot wind, and no rain for months. All felt it on their faces with the sweat and smut, knowing with sinking hearts that the weather was against them.

Some had escaped by water, pushing their vessels into the Gulf. How many had floated off into the darkness, squinting against the smoke as they watched embers fall in showers above their heads, wondering, every one of them, what might afterwards remain?

The wharf was still there, and the famous White Tower, but flames had leapt to moored boats that were now a sludge on black water. This too was one of the beauties, the ocean aglow with scattered light, and for all that was lost and char, there were the modest boats, the small fishing vessels of the poor, that slid their neat shapes away and carried their human cargo to safety.

Every now and then came an explosion: stored oil, possibly armaments.

The people of Salonika streamed from the centre, stumbling across rough flagstones. Under flicker, under shroud, they gathered their lives and left. Some hauled carpets; some carried mirrors or sewing machines. Their voices blew upwards in snatches, collective in their panic.

William T. Wood, of Putney, renowned for his paintings of English flowers, was appointed war artist for the Balkans in the First World War. He favoured pale pinks, yellows and mauves, and painted the 'Great Fire' of Salonika as he witnessed it from an observation balloon in August 1917. It was a morning-after scene, brightly calm, with a floaty view from the heavens. In his signature pastels, remote as a child's dream and thinly decorative, he painted smoke wafting in floral cumulus above the stricken city. There were no visible human or animal figures. Testimony, he called it, proud of the composition and the palette, and smugly pleased to have painted a Big Event.

But this was the first night, and fire was still a surprise. Shapes were dark against carnival colours and the wind gave everything a quality of animation.

Those who viewed Wood's painting later, in London, saw the pretty lies of art.

Former residents and soldiers said, No, it wasn't like that.

Eventually, tired of the spectacle, the men of the Allied Army of the Orient and the British Salonika Force returned to their camp. None spoke a word now. What was the point? It was like the silence after dragging bodies from no-man's-land back to the trenches. There was nothing to say. There was nothing to meet the huge moment. They returned by instinct to drear duty and mechanical movement, to their slower and heavier selves, listing with exhaustion and ready to fold inwards. Excitement left and in its place was a murky lugging of spirit. The men extinguished their fag ends and saved them in their pockets and the toes of their boots. The scale of importance shifted; to imagine a ciggie first thing and a hot mug of tea at dawn.

Feverish, unquiet, they slept on straw pallets, calling out, as soldiers do, or tossing and turning in dreamland, their allied heads full of malaria and foreign fire.

HER FACE WAS black and her eyes were smarting but something had lit inside her.

Olive was there with her ambulance lorry, helping the evacuation. Beneath towering smoke and falling ash she worked methodically, taking sixteen souls at a time, mostly the aged and the frail. Her vehicle could not enter the city centre, so she met civilians as they fled. They towed handcarts, whipped famished donkeys, loaded themselves with meagre treasures and small crying children, and all were alike in their generalised fear. Olive tended them and offered water, though it was in short supply. She poured a little into each mouth, then bundled those she could fit into her lorry. Some had a balm of oil wiped on their burns. They glowed with sore lustre but did not complain. Faces were upturned in appeal, eyes carried the glitter of the fire. They reeked of sweat and smoke, made sour with the dirty air.

To and fro Olive went, unrelieved, for twenty hours. By the end her hands could no longer hold the steering wheel. They were stiff as a corpse and clumsy as claws, and though she rubbed at her fingers, they did not open and clasp as they should. She leant against the long gearstick, forced the machine to shudder forward, felt her feet work at the clutch and plunge down on the resisting accelerator.

All the power she'd once possessed, when she first began driving, was now this urging into darkness, pulling at the choke, forcing lorry-life into the mass of lazy metal around her. She could feel the wheels churning away, finding traction with the heavy load. In the rear-view mirror exhaust met the smoke of a dying city.

And when at last she stopped, back at the field of tents that composed the Scottish Women's Hospital, she fell immediately asleep. It was voluptuous to sink at last, bone-tired and released, with no need to remove her boots or uniform. She fell into the stink of a burnt, irrecoverable world. There would be nothing for a while but pitch-black and smoke in her clothes and hair. But she was burning in her dream as a myth might burn. She was falling like Icarus, transformed into a story.

GRACE WAS A surgeon working with the Scottish Women's Hospital. She moved slowly in the tent as she checked the dressings of an amputee. The soldier could not have been more than twenty, from Cardiff, someone said, David, someone said, when they heard him mumble in broken Welsh at the height of his delirium.

Yes, definitely Welsh. His face was bare and childish, his voice sounded clotted and strangled. The friend who had brought him in looked on with tender dismay— love, perhaps, men's love—and whispered encouraging endearments, such as a mother might offer to a feverish babe.

The Welshman and his compatriot. We are representatives, Grace thought. War has made us both less and more than what we are. This man, his bandages bloody, his stumps poking towards her as if in accusation: legless but national, a child and a hero. If he made it home he would signify 'war wounded' and 'unlucky bastard' to those who watched as he begged, or dragged, or sat perched on a mobile thatched chair, perhaps bearing a placard at his chest that read 'Balkans Service'.

She smelt the smoke of Salonika, blown across miles. Before night fell she saw a ridge of airborne ash, then in darkness a vermilion glow like a welt on the horizon. Already she'd heard the story of three cats, flung burning from a building by an old crone who refused to move. It seemed credible enough, to fling creatures away, to save pets when one was too worn-out to budge. One cat was a ball of fire, they said.

Later Grace would note the details in her diary: two cats saved, one lost, while an old woman perished in rising flames. A man called David who would certainly die that night. And an ancient city made ash; and yet more refugees on the way.

She readied herself for burnt bodies and no sleep. She thought: *Antisepsis, bacteriostasis, debridement.* In France she'd dealt almost daily with burn pathology, those hurt from bombs, grenades and rockets; and the chemicals: chlorine, phosgene, mustard gas.

How variously men contrive to murder each other.

Grace organised morphine and checked the sterilisation of dressings. She superintended the preparation of iodine, brandy and paraffin wax. She stopped only for a cigarette, puffing with dull vacancy and lack of pleasure.

It was after midnight. Such a peaceful time, not yet hectic with arrivals of the newly burnt or wounded. Grace looked at David's face, now still and silent, now closed into his dying. Courteously, like a servant, she pulled the blanket to his chin.

STELLA WORKED AS assistant cook in the hospital kitchen. This is what they gave to a writer volunteering, the most menial of jobs. So many potatoes to peel, and so little meat. Her fingers were blistered from opening cans of brownish meaty stuff, muck by another name. For the Australians working at the hospital, this was an insult to the spirit. She was sick of the giant pots that she stirred with a stick, and the smell of old cabbage and something grey and rancid. She was cranky and wanting more: amusement, mutton stew, a gramophone, new books. Her favourite task was distributing tobacco on Sundays. The patients were all so pathetically grateful. They reached up to her with pained smiles and skinny fingers, stretching beyond their ruined faces and bandaged limbs to accept her gift.

'Sister!' they called out, as if she too was a nurse and deserved respect.

But now she was sparked by the fire and its implausible magnitude. Afterwards, she heard that it burned for thirty-two hours. She heard how little the residents of Salonika wept, and how stoically they moved on. Seventy thousand people lost their homes. There would be a new tent city nearby, and more sent away on trains, to other cities and other tents, refugees at a time of ever more refugees. The hospital tents were already at capacity and she

9

saw their triangular shapes in the moonlight. This was the condition of everything now, an impermanence of homes and borders, vanquished dreams, tough loss, living and dying beneath a thin, fluttery membrane of canvas.

It was hard not to think in these terms of historical summation. Hard not to see it all unending and too large to be solved. Not the Kaiser this time, not the Bulgar or the Fritz, but ordinary error and elemental destruction.

Later Stella heard that the Hagia Sophia remained intact, standing where it had stood, unburnt, from the early eighth century.

Irreligious, she was unsure why this news had so moved her.

STANLEY, A YOUNG artist, volunteered as a medical orderly with the Royal Army Medical Corps in 1915. He'd done ten months in a hospital in Bristol, six weeks in Field Ambulance training, and now he was ready for action. He arrived at Salonika on the troopship *Llandovery Castle*, amused that a ship was named for a castle, considering the anomaly of rock and ocean, thinking of his four older brothers, already at the Front, and wondering if they knew that he was now on active service. Royal Berkshire Regiment.

A small man, with red ears, owlish spectacles and a nervy disposition, he was unsuited to soldiering but wished fervently for adventure. He was one of those who stood that first night watching the city burn, feeling rather ashamed of his pleasure, and confused by Salonika gleaming lovely before him, flashing its own demise.

As he watched, he thought about the citizens of the city and made his own stories. A family, how they would have smelt the smoke for hours, foolishly calm at first, rising from a late supper, then known at last that they must leave. Children at play in the street, stopping to gaze at the sky, then running inside, coughing and afraid. Or a lover, leaving a bed, washing away stickiness with water from a jug on the sideboard, seeing the orange glow at the window and realising that the blaze was beyond control.

Ah, the lovers. There would have been panic, and the man or woman in the bed would have rushed to retrieve clothes and hastily dress, so they could head together down crooked stairs and out onto the street, only half aware that this was the end of all that they cherished.

How he wished to paint it. The razed city. The human drama. He saw the old forms broken, shaped in new alignments, the destructible world abstracted in splendid innovations. He would paint the couple on the bed, made tired and saggy by their lovemaking, sprawled together in naked, ungainly relaxation; beyond them the orange window before they both saw and knew. Already he understood the power of derangement, and how a single window might contain an entire fate.

SOMETIMES SHE MISSED it: Sydney with its ferries and shops and checking the gin for afternoon tennis. The great harbour richly swelling, rendered scenic for the wealthy. The maid with a tray, her fanned cap perky, her sluttish habit of twirling her hair. It was always late afternoon, the air sleepy and awash in ochre light.

Olive was untying her tennis shoes when she decided she must leave. Her dress was adhesive with sweat, her face rosy with winning and flirtation, when she felt dissatisfaction move like a tremor through her body. She scarcely knew what it was, so accustomed to having all she needed. She saw her own narrow hand holding her gaping shoe and wondered what, if anything, she might do with her useless life.

She flapped at her collar to cool herself, lifted her damp hair from her sweltering neck and downed a gin and tonic, minus tinkling ice. But still the feeling remained. A useless life. A mere passing through. She'd read in books of such moments: an interception of self-knowledge that required a rapid change, a Victorian lady glimpsing the truth of her marriage in a gilded doorway, or of another's deception, or of general iniquity; then swishing balloon skirts as she fled along Italianate halls. But this was the twentieth century, 1913, and Olive was entirely modern and heedless.

She banged her shoes together and shook them as if they contained sand. She looked across at the white sails leaning on the blue harbour, jiggling, aslant, pulled by wind towards the ocean. Beyond the cliffs lay the Pacific, beating its meaningless repetition.

Olive's father, a widowed banker, had given her a pampered start. By both conviction and means he believed in excess in all things material. Even their potted ferns were too big, flourishing madly, and she would recall them with a mixture of nostalgia and revulsion. These ferns were her father's hobby; he liked to stroke their long arms, snip at ailing fronds, squirt a little water and then fondle the soil to check the quality of damp. Daily he performed this task, with dozens of indoor ferns. The rooms of their house were dank green, the affectation one of jungle. The rich, Olive learned early, are permitted cheery eccentricity; ordinary people must suffer cheerless constraint.

Afternoon breezes set off the tiniest ruffle of sound, as if plants in their brass urns were speaking leaf language together, sending messages across the parquetry, communing around the fringed standing-lamps and plush-covered chairs.

Olive regarded her father with condescension as she

stepped barefoot into the green drawing room. She swung her tennis shoes, tied by the laces, in a gesture contrived to annoy.

He asked about her game; she told him the score. There was no novelty in this conversation for father and daughter, only practised lines, languid as ping-pong, dodging the ferns. Then she announced her intention to leave.

Father barely blinked. 'You'll need a chaperone, a new trunk and letters of introduction.'

It might have been his own dream, to up and leave.

'Just money,' Olive responded. And they both knew what she meant. Money was everything. He'd spent a life-time telling her so. The ferns in unison seemed vigorously to nod.

It was a conspiracy between them. Olive said she would stay in London with her older sister, Violet, since 'London' had an inviolable probity and prestige. It meant glamorous relatives, serious shopping and monumental history. It meant poise, the right hat, a smoothing of colonial vowels, submission to papery aunts, crisp and folded. But Germany was her true destination. She'd spent a year in Dresden being 'finished' at the age of fifteen and now longed to return.

Olive was still in London when war broke out. Her wealth allowed her to imagine adventure, not trenches. Predictably, Violet had married a banker, but Olive wanted no such domestic destiny, no gentleman named Alfred in Kensal Green, buttoning his grey tweed waistcoat in the wide hall mirror, adjusting his rabbit-hair trilby, taking his umbrella from the elephant's foot stand by the doorway, hanging it on his arm fixedly, as if he too was inanimate. Olive watched this early morning ritual with distaste.

There was a baby coming and Olive recoiled from her sister's body. Violet sensed her contempt. She turned her face to her sister, saying: 'Scottish Women's Hospital? You? You have not a single skill.'

She could drive. She had money. Money was everything. She bought a lorry fitted out to become an ambulance. Her father bankrolled her endeavour, enjoying his own war-effort largesse. Olive thought of him standing over his ferns, admiring their relentless unfurling. She saw him dawdling in his greenhouse, with sunlight dropping in splotches, as he inspected the rubbery fingers of new life arranged row by row in wee pots.

He favoured her above her sister and was generous to a fault.

She was different now. War had remade her. Her ambulance had remade her. She had extended into its metal body and become resolute and strong. Her own body was the innards of a large machine, and she was proud of her efficiency and aptitude for hard work. A year driving her ambulance in France had taught her guarded, cunning habits, so that her fondness for her father and Violet was a deeply private matter. In the context of calamity, she must hold her family apart.

She had not expected to see the aberration of her times so close. Nor for the war to go on and on. Now she was a volunteer in yet another wretched country, still transporting the maimed and the dead.

On the first night of the Great Fire of Salonika, through all the weary hours, Olive drove automatically. People banged on the side of her lorry, when she was already full. Called out. Wanted attention. Begged for water. There was too much to do and too many distressed, and she was aware of pushing past the desperate and imploring. She kept the motor running, idling in a low grumble. Through the windscreen she saw the city flare upwards and collapse. In her machine full to bursting, she pulled away.

Most of the rescued she would not remember. They were as so many bent shapes, piling into the ambulance. But at some stage in the long night she noticed a particular old man. He wore a white skullcap and was bronze and erect. When he wedged himself towards the back of her lorry, she saw that he held a mirror between his legs. He leant forward, as if in prayer, as if in supplication to the Fates, but was simply protecting his mirror in the clasp of his knees. Later it occurred to Olive he wanted the proof of reflection, to see himself still whole.

When at last she was alone, she extracted a cigarette, rolled earlier, from the pocket of her uniform. Regardless of the smoky air Olive wanted more smoke. Her arms were stiff, her fingers inflexible, so she wedged the cigarette and bent her face towards it like a wounded soldier. She inhaled as if she was a daytripper by the seaside, filling up her lungs with fresh blue life.

TRUTH BE TOLD, Grace resented eight of her nine brothers. She was the third, incongruous child, and the only daughter. When little, she suspected that she had other parents somewhere, that she was the neglected special girl, from another, secret family. Even as an adult she felt misfitted and mostly alone.

In dreams her brothers lined up in descending size, each in a bowler hat and black overcoat, tyrannical in their uniformity. Years later, when she saw René Magritte's *Golconda*, in which men in bowler hats rain down (or float up) over a nondescript beige city, she saw there with startled recognition the truth of the matter, that mass of behatted men who patterned the world, paradoxically both falling and rising, populating even the sky. She loved only the brother closest to her in age, the handsome second, Gerald. Exempting Gerald, men were tiresome, even as they bowed before her, offering courtly flourishes with insincere smirks, fatuous in conversation, tedious in taste if not ambition, smarmy, false. She grew up surrounded by such men. She began lost and outnumbered, but ended found and determined.

Born in 1883, at St Leonards-on-Sea, Grace knew the contradiction of the glory of the ocean and her suffocating family. Her parents were of the Plymouth Brethren, strictly unloving and cruelly pious. Father showed a vague interest, which she found oppressive. Mother was remote but critical, and ignored all her children, apart from the eldest and favourite son, James. Any female prestige, alongside nine brothers, did not transpire. She might have been a stray kitten wandered in for milk, so little regard was paid her. James often lay in their mother's bed, and Grace remembered him nestling into her body, as if claiming sole ownership. His possession was unrivalled and he nurtured his mother's religious mania. Grace imagined him at her death, enveloped in those huge bovine breasts.

As soon as she could, she left the family behind. Impatient to change, Grace was precocious from the start. She studied hard. Made herself manly. Endured the stodgy food of Newcastle so that she could take her medical degree, then outshone all the men in her surgical training. She was openly contemptuous of those who quaked before a stinky cadaver or hesitated with the first, nervous incision of the scalpel. The material body was obligingly inert; she was reassured that beneath all the tumult of emotions there was this constant, solid flesh and its scientific description. Organs in their place, ailments in categories, the cause-and-effect business of diagnosis and treatment. The first glimpses inside were such a surprise: how like meat the body was, how fatty, how soulless, how vulnerable to decay. Gristle, what an awful word, not elegant, like ligament. The crimson too had shocked her, that she might be so colourful inside this pale oyster flesh.

Only Gerald was dear. In letters he discussed with her the intimate disappointments of their family. She guessed her brother was a sodomite, and doomed to be miserable and wifeless, but this drew them closer, what was known and not said. Law and religion had condemned him to perversion and Grace felt likewise perverse. He wrote of his special friendships with new chums and she wished she could similarly boast, or say that she had found money, or status, or some divine equilibrium that enabled her to attach to another with the jubilant intensity of love. But what she had found was work. Useful work.

After two years of the horrors of France, Macedonia was an easier commission. No longer in the shelter of a stone abbey, overwhelmed by blast and gas victims, she found that tent life in the middle of nowhere oddly suited her. The tent hospital was further from England and more open and unpredictable. There was an austerity that inclined her to new ideas of freedom. The shell-like light of afternoon, the dry country beyond, the flap and tremble of canvas above her as she slept: these composed a new immediacy in what had been a too busy life. Urgent work was more intermittent; this too suited her. To have fewer patients, more time, space each day to read and to think.

Grace moved slowly through the after-midnight hush inside the tent. The hot wind conveyed a bodily vibration. There was a slippery quality to the light, the sense of an easy shift between shadows and illumination that she took irrationally to be a distinctive quality of hospital spaces. The dark was darker, especially here, where death was tucked close. The light from their lamps, always of poor quality, was at times guttering and thin. She found she must tilt her notes to read.

She would check soon to see if David was still alive but allowed him his indeterminate status a little longer. Alive, not alive. There were random shouts, though most of the men were asleep or bleary with medication. David was quiet and settled.

From outside, she could hear a soldier on lookout duty softly singing 'Mademoiselle from Armentières'. The soldier's tone was dazed and disconnected, as if forcing himself to stay awake, even as he enjoyed the sound of his own voice.

Grace listened to the verses, which became more obscene as the song progressed. Mademoiselle was lusty and imprecise enough to contain any man's fantasy.

Before the song finished she understood without looking that the Welsh boy had died. She could have saved herself the trouble of surgical amputation and knew as she performed it that he had the early symptoms of malaria and ought not, in that condition, to have been put under the knife. It was for the loving man at David's side that she had tried for a miracle. It was an error, certainly, a professional error. What had she been thinking? She had risked her authority. She had spoilt her own record. She had made the mistake of imagining beyond the brute red stuff of the body. It was a decision that she would strive to forget. In this place, with these men, and some in extremity, there were 'errors of attention' that meant wounds were sometimes misjudged or the treatment a mistake and a waste. She did not write 'errors of attention' on the death certificate. She made no record of what might later condemn her.

Grace summoned an orderly to deal with the disposal of the body. Her duty now was to write to the family. In her years of service she had developed a rhetorical style that remade inglorious death, and for which her religious education supplied words of sacrifice and redemption. So to her professional mistake she added the sin of mendacity. She erased the boy-soldier David, whose bloody wounds, like those of all amputees, smelt to her mysteriously of nasturtiums, who was a jolting lump, carried in by someone who cared, who called out in Welsh to summon his mother or lover, who was an unlucky bugger tricked to believe he might usefully kill, or be killed.

She dared not consider if her letters offered comfort, or none. No time for that. No time at all. She saw the companion cry, then rise, then flee from the tent. She noticed that he kept trailing his fingers through his hair, feeling the contours of his own skull as if to soothe what was raging inside.

WHEN SHE HEARD of the rubble, and the city of Salonika burning, Stella was reminded of San Francisco in 1906. She had arrived there by boat from Australia only twelve days after the earthquake, and it was her first trip abroad, to seek her own meaning. She left within days, dismayed by the ruins, the despair and the sense of hope overturned. She rode in a pony trap down Market Street, her carpet bag bobbing, and realised that she had imagined an imperishable world, one which acknowledged and included her. But this was a city destroyed. Everyone was coping with shatter and loss. The small hotel she had booked was half gone when she arrived, just a façade standing in front of a pile of bricks, and the addled proprietor sitting in the dust with his head in his hands. Gutted buildings, soldiers cleaning, tent cities springing up. The city hall, its ornate cupola still standing high above its own ruin, looked eerie and indicative of the end of the world. Whole blocks had burned down and made the city a black, stinking chaos.

She would recall brick dust in the air, and the lingering smoke from the fires, and the way grit entered her mouth and the tight folds of her bodice and skirt.

She had climbed over a fallen wall to check if there was a dead body behind it. She'd convinced herself she would find a corpse, a child, or an old woman. There was no body behind the wall. No child or old woman. What was she doing there?

Decisive, Stella bought a train ticket east. There was no point staying, and San Francisco didn't want her. What could be more alien than an Australian woman, motivated by unionism and women's rights, wandering distrait in a ruined city?

On the train, Stella was hazy and without energy, going where she was taken. She sped into America, barely looking as the new land flicked and skittered alongside her.

She forgot her hatbox and left it on the train. When she arrived in Chicago, she walked around hatless for days, her high hairdo flying apart in the vicious wind. She felt maddened, colonial and stupidly conspicuous.

Now, more than a decade later, she was a different woman, internationalised and sure. She was a journalist and a writer, though the fame she sought eluded her. In London, she found work in the Minerva Café on High Holborn, and this was enough to recommend her for a six-month contract with the Scottish Women's Hospital: 'assistant cook and orderly'. In truth, she barely knew a pot from a pan, and had to ask an Irish biddy to give her a few tips. Potatoes, she learned, will satisfy any craving and are by far the easiest foodstuff to prepare.

Stella had expected France and its publicised dramas, and was disappointed to be assigned to a tent hospital near the lesser-known Eastern Front. But the place suited her. She grew to enjoy the dove light of early mornings and the rough appeal of a more foreign country. She liked to wake before the sun to see the snow-capped mountain in the distance, gradually becoming pale yellow with the climbing dawn. Sycamores, elms, purple hills rolling away, a tang in the summer air of olives and grapes. Dry wind, mottled tarpaulins catching a steep slope of sunlight. It was peaceful at the hospital camp at Ostrovo, with the lake nearby, at the foot of Mount Kaimakchalan, and far enough from the Front.

This was the night of the fire, and very late. The burns patients they'd prepared for had yet to arrive, and the soldiers, French, Serbian and British, were fitfully asleep. Mostly malaria, but a few seriously wounded from a recent bombardment. Now and then, a soldier called out. In whatever language they called, it was always the same: Oh my God! No! Sometimes: Mother! *Maman!*

The usual, Stella thought.

The usual half-conscious outrage at the war and seeing bodies blown asunder. The usual calling for a mother. When she first arrived it had been one of the difficult things to get used to: the way grown men shouted like children under the cover of darkness and sleep.

Stella recalled her hatbox, still lamented, and the hats stacked inside it. One in particular, trimmed with posies of Parma violets fashioned in satiny cloth. The bitter smell of cinders sweeping through the train, and the stations all alike, with peaked roofs and tin signals and roughly blown bunting. The anxiety and disappointment with which she had fled. Curious it was, how memories of lost things seemed to follow her.

The lamplight in the tent was brown and subdued. The canvas above their heads was lightly swaying. Apart from the smoke in the air, it was a routine night and unusually calm. From outside, Stella heard the low voice of a soldier on duty:

> Oh, Mademoiselle from Armentières
> Parlay-voo
> She's the hardest working girl in town
> But she makes her living upside down
> Inky pinky parlay-voo

Oh, Mademoiselle from Armentières
Parlay-voo
She'll do it for wine, she'll do it for rum
And sometimes for chocolate or chewing gum
Inky pinky parlay-voo

Stella was inexperienced and a little afraid of such songs. Men wanted only one thing: that was what she had been told for years. But she waited to hear the whole song, right up to the cunts and the tits, and blushed for her fear and all she did not understand. She stood a while smoothing her uniform, pulling and pressing it down, regaining her composure.

At the end of the tent the surgeon was examining a man with no legs. Grace bent above him and touched his brow with the back of her hand as if checking for a fever, but it was clear even to Stella that the amputee was already gone. Not just stillness, but indefinable vacancy hovered around the dim spot where he lay propped. Beside the stretcher another man, bandaged across the chest and with visible contusions on his face, began soft weeping. In between sobs he spoke fragments of a language she learned later was Welsh.

The weeping man rose and stumbled for the tent opening, pushing past her as he went. He gave a great sniff. Stella saw the shame in his face, a kind of inward ferocity, and the damp flush of his cheeks as he lowered his head to hide the overflow of feeling. He rubbed his fingers through his spiked hair and looked a mess.

This was another early lesson. Death brought mostly silence and a locking down of response. But some of the soldiers were truly unmanned. They sank into blubber and embarrassment, then enacted gestures of loss and displacement—searching for some apparently casual item, a comb, a pair of spectacles, a letter thrust into a pocket. The confusion of death misplaced everything, even a comb.

WHEN STANLEY WAS at the Slade School of Fine Art, he learned of post-impressionist relativity and the radical dissolve of images into colour. Daub as the truth of things.

When, a few years later, he was summoned in early morning to still-burning Salonika, there was a ghastly toughness to the real world and the dissolve was only by flame.

The heat was infernal and more than once he thought that he would faint. He found himself squatting like a schoolboy at marbles, trying to disguise his dizzy fear, noticing as he did so the intricate patterns in the flag-stones. It was in his nature, had always been, this sense that the world contained its own pictures.

His head throbbed and he felt he was close to tears. So much destruction. Black ruins stood like a haunting behind his spectacles. Buildings scorched and broken crowded and surrounded him.

But Stanley did his bit, helping to fight the fire, though resources were scarce. There were a few fire stations, but these belonged to private insurance compa-nies, and owed their business only to the insured. Most of the water, in any case, had long been siphoned to the army camps and had to be laboriously trucked back to the city. The soldiers' job was to locate small wells and domestic tanks. In several languages Stanley heard lingo which meant *Water! Water!*

Someone found hoses that winemakers used to fill up their barrels; they sprayed wine-scented water on objects piled in the street—chairs, carpets, painted ikons in frames—and splashed feebly at anything else that looked wooden or combustible. They were disconcerting, those soaking piles, one with a child's handcart of woven cane-work, another topped by a brass bedstead, another wholly, and inexplicably, built from carefully stacked mirrors. Stanley's artist eye could not resist the ordinary grandeur there—the shifting angles and surfaces, the facets of gold from reflections. A small dog running past was doubled in a streak of light. The legs of a mule, flashing as in the slots of a zoetrope. Cut-up versions of labouring men.

Angle, not daub.

Other soldiers, those from the Western Front, were worldly wise. They had travelled; they had already seen towns reduced to smoking rubble. But Stanley was new to the field, and this was his first time abroad. He was still agog at fluted sandstone, classical shapes and ornate inscriptions. For all the ash, this too was a holy land.

'Holy land,' he insisted, to anyone who would listen.

St Paul, no less, wrote Epistles to the Thessalonians, had preached here, stayed faithful.

Stanley had read of Macedonia in Herodotus and retained his art-student admiration for classical books. He knew his Greek myths. He knew of Alexander the Great.

His friend George, also of the Berkshire Regiment, lightly teased him. 'Will it make a difference, if we die here, knowing this geezer came before us?' He offered a grim little laugh.

It was not a question that Stanley could hope to answer. Though it might be commonplace, he was appalled by the destruction of what appeared old, and by the loss of sacred buildings, synagogues, churches and mosques.

'They're ancient,' he said, as if there was nothing more to add, as if antiquity won any argument.

George had a misshapen face, skewed to one side as if pushed, and yellow hair that stood upright, cartoonishly shocked. Others in the regiment disregarded or mocked him. This was the basis of their friendship: two outsiders. George was a good soul, Stanley decided, and they liked each other. Both were shy, unmanly.

Before them stood the remains of a smouldering mosque, its dome caved in at the top, its minarets upright but smoking. Threads of smoke rose everywhere, issuing from ribbed curves and fallen stone. A handful of fez-hatted worshippers, one bandaged at the jaw, wandered around the ruin, looking for who knew what. One man had a walking stick with which he uselessly prodded. There were no women present. This was a world without women.

George removed his helmet to wipe his brow, and his hair sprang again into comedy style.

Everywhere Stanley saw versions of his own orthodoxies and symbols. He would not relinquish them. A bearded man in long robes, clutching a Torah, materialised from nowhere to hobble past. It was like a scene from biblical times, the scroll clasped at the chest and across the shoulder, the cedar handles, handsomely bulbous, poking out at each end, the air of solemnity in guarding something entirely beyond value. New recruits clasped their rifles in exactly this way. He could not resist the comparison, and the similarity pained and dismayed him.

A boy, perhaps eight or nine years old, sidled up to Stanley to sell a postcard-sized ikon of a saint. He held out his hand and made the universal gesture of touching his mouth in hunger, then rubbed at his belly for extra measure. He was filthy and anaemic and terribly thin. He

34

had a gaping harelip. Stanley recoiled. He thrust coins towards the boy but could not bear to look at his face, or at the image in his palm. The child moved away to offer it to another.

A barrel burst and the narrow street filled with red wine. Then someone smashed a second barrel open with a rifle butt. George threw himself onto the road, along with other Tommies and Frogs, and Stanley watched as the men lapped like dogs from wine pooling in the grooved gutters. George lifted his head, amused, gave a thumbs-up sign, and added a theatrical wink before he returned to his slurping. The wine merchant, frantic and cross, was scooping the dregs with petrol tins, but it was a hopeless task. Five or six men were on their bellies, their greedy mouths wine-dark, their uniforms guiltily stained. The little boy with the ikon was there too, lapping with the men. His small form looked from behind as if he had fallen into a red lake and drowned. A few onlookers watched the drinkers with evident scorn. Stanley could hear in their voices that they felt as he did, that like him they shrank with disgust. Gutter-filthy wine and a pervasive smell of rot.

There were also lootings and shootings. Stanley didn't see this himself, but their captain announced later, unconvincingly, that no Tommy soldier had been involved. Two French privates were arrested for stealing jewels and attempting to sell them. They would be court-martialled and shot. Let this be a warning. The degenerate Frogs, the captain joked, *Les Poilus*, he sneered, deliberately mispronouncing so that they all laughed uneasily. Dagoes too were found stealing and had been dealt 'rough justice'. No discipline at all, not like the British. Not like the dependable Tommy. No one mentioned the men drunk in the streets and the way they'd been pushed onto lorries and hidden away. Or the mistreated whores, or the violations that every soldier saw.

Poor Stanley thought that his head would explode. He could see facets of innovative vision announcing themselves before him, how angles made new the existence of the world, and how ill-fitted he was to this life of rough, cynical men.

His home village had lanes and flowery hedges and women with hats and cane baskets. Postboxes. Corner shops. Swan-upping on the river. He remembered the civility of their daily hallos, flattened, it was true, by years of habit and safety, but also in their own way beatific and sound. So many flowers: hydrangeas, freesias, cornflowers, pansies, all of them painterly, particular, notations of mixed colour. Shell-pink or lemon roses, dropping a litter of blown petals, the soft cheeks of sweet peas. He had taken it all for granted. He loved the charming artlessness of a woman holding knitting and a ball of yarn in her lap, or a child bending in pure kindness to feed a stray cat. He was a man who, witnessing the public disgrace of his fellows, relied on the integrity of sentimental and simple things.

The soldiers were marched back quick smart after the ineffectual dousing.

Stanley's head was still throbbing. It was the foul air, perhaps, or early malaria, or the mighty effort to manage his despair and sense of self-righteousness.

Behind them Salonika continued its unmaking. Smoke hung in a dark thunderhead above the wreck of the city, advertising that the drama was yet unfinished. Stragglers were here and there returning to salvage what might remain. A small group of men appeared on the dusty road, their faces gloomy and powdered with ash. All were hunched and bore a look of collective bereavement.

The boy with the ikon plunged past them. He was stained red and running with an urgency that implied he'd seen something fatal. Dirty legs, impossibly thin, rushing away in a blur. Boy became shadow. Shadow became burnt something. Burnt something a busted building, hollowed out and emitting black smoke.

Stanley kept removing his glasses to clean them.

Now, dear God, he didn't quite trust what he saw.

AH, FINGERS.

Olive woke from her deep sleep to discover that her hands were flexible and revived. In seconds she recalled the long day and night before, when she had driven the ambulance to and from the fire and seen the spectacle of Salonika burning. The refugees were now being dispersed into tent cities or triaged in the clearing stations and field hospitals of the allied forces. She lay still for a full minute, feeling pleased with herself. This was a necessary moment, this stillness, to gather her body back, to find her outlines again, and her warm fleshy substance. To return from whatever otherworld that deep sleep had been.

Now tea. Olive would seek a mug of tea. She parted the mosquito net, sat up, hung her legs from the side of her stretcher and considered herself with a critical grunt. Her clothes stank, and when she removed her socks she found that her feet were foetid and repulsive. In France she'd seen men whose feet had been bloated by months of standing in water, who had spongy forms like sea creatures where their toes and heels had once been, one man who could not stand bootless without crying. Trench foot, they called it. The crying man had looked down in such desolate puzzlement: after trench life, avoiding blasts, seeing his regiment gassed and exploded, he had to deal with this marine transformation. Twenty years old, that man was, and he had lost his feet.

Olive changed her socks swiftly, superstitiously, then blew under her sweaty arms. She splashed her grimy face in a basin of shallow water. A swim in the lake would do it, with a few other women from the hospital. She looked forward to immersion, and release from her own sour stink.

They had swum from time to time, but there were the mosquitoes to consider. More soldiers died here of malaria than were killed by the Germans and Bulgars. She pulled on her long gloves and checked her socks. In the evenings she was obliged like the nurses to enter net-world and cover her face. They moved masked to each other, peering beyond circular veils that resembled those worn by beekeepers.

Fucking mozzies.

Summer was the worst, and only last month another of their nurses had succumbed, sent off to the hospital in Salonika to die. The hospital had no doubt burned along with the shops and the glamorous Palais de Variété restaurant. She blocked her speculation there, not wanting to think of patients caught helpless in a burning building, in a devastated city.

It was not something they spoke of.

Yesterday, Olive had eaten only a tin of sardines, forked with greasy fingers and gulped in a rush, standing behind her lorry. Now she was hungry. The so-called cook, Stella, handed her a mug of tea and a slab of dark bread.

'Christmas!'

This was a humour she understood. She scoffed with unseemly, unladylike haste. The tea was sweet and strong and the bread smeared with a salty, greyish fat that tasted of anchovy. Stella smiled her approval of the hearty scoff and announced she'd been pleased to learn that Olive had finally returned, and was not injured, or missing, or ill.

'Thought you'd gone walkabout!'

Stella was known for her slang. Brown spots of iodine speckled her broad face. Olive imagined her sleeping beneath a tear in the mosquito net or venturing forgetful into the night without her cover. She looked vulnerable and Olive felt a rush of affection. Now, back at the hospital, she could allow herself feelings.

Stella hoisted the huge blackened teapot and left to dispense more cups of tea. It would be another hot day; already, she was flushed.

No banter this morning, Stella was too busy. There were days with banter, there were days without.

Olive took a quick piss in the latrine, then found a seat on a tin drum outside the mess tent and rolled a cigarette. Two. She enjoyed the ritual, the delicate spreading of the strands of tobacco, the cradling and rolling of the tissue paper, the soft, precise lick. Patting at the ends, removing a wisp from the tongue. There was the tiny wait for the fizz when the flame caught, and the first deep inhalation. Somewhere at her core she felt the nicotine sear, and with it the welcome, crackly burn. This was a kind of peace. She had learned to take peace when it came, and now she could look at the mountain and the glint of the lake and the tent shapes bright in the morning sun.

A smoky breeze surfed the grasses and fluttered the tents; beyond that, far distant, a haze hung low in the sky, indicating Salonika and evidence of what might otherwise have seemed imaginary.

Hard to believe what lay beyond, and all that had been ruined. Olive had driven along roads piling with stone and seen buildings judder alight, like living bodies. Tram wires hung loose; burnt-out cars were smoking shells. Monuments were scattered into bricks and marble. She saw a cracked mosaic showing a dim Byzantine story. A melancholy face and sprig of lily, a figure in a robe, meekly kneeling. She wondered what century she had seen, and what form of desecration fire connoted. Or what kind of worship.

By the harbour there were boats reduced to shapeless waste, floating on the sullied waters of the Thermaic Gulf.

The ruins in France made more sense, since shelling was war after all, but this was a local disaster and unexpected. Most of the nurses had forged a connection with the city, since occasionally, like the officer class, they were allowed to visit. They were given safe passage through the 'birdcage' of barbed wire that formed its border, and most had visited the post office, or the White Tower, or had assignations at a café. For Olive, Salonika was proof of gorgeous miscellany, Ottoman polyglot culture, the metropolitan world. Not to mention cinema, sweets, access to alcohol.

She saved her fag end, as she had seen men do. She placed it carefully in her chest pocket, alongside the other cigarette. You never knew when you might need this direct kind of comfort. Nurses placed cigarettes in the mouths of dying men, thinking to ease them into mental passivity, or the rest and recreation of another place. In fuggy semi-dark, breathing Capstan or Woodbine, tasting the last burn in their nostrils and throats, they became corpses, not men.

There was something gruesome in seeing a cigarette alive in the mouth of the dead. Once she'd been the one to pluck the butt away, and found herself twisting her heel into the dirt as if it had been a scorpion.

At that moment, Olive felt most tired of the war. When she took a lit cigarette from a rumpled, dead face and knew she would not want a ciggie that night, but a bromide and her own obliteration.

GRACE REMEMBERED WHEN once, illicitly, she had sea-bathed at Hastings. Her family religion would not permit such a practice. It was a desire of the body, an indulgence and theologically unsound. But she had been staying with liberal relations, testing her skills as a medic even then, at fourteen, by helping to care for a dying great-aunt. Her cousin, the beautiful Ruth, three years her senior, had persuaded her to don a bathing costume.

For all her strength of character, Grace was more afraid than excited. Such a huge space to encompass a girl. Under no one's control, the sea water surged and retracted, and there was no end to it, really, no limit to what, in her fear, was a commitment of the body to danger. Shingles loosened beneath her toes. Light reached in shafts to her pallid feet. The tide rippled in and surface sheen parted and lapped around her.

Yet it was a kind of elation to feel the creep of cold up her body. Her clammy bloomers moulded to her shape and she began, with a buoyancy of step, to be tugged and swept. Ruth held her firmly and taught her how to float on her back, then how to hold her nose and put her face under the water. Ruth grasped her at the waist and offered words of encouragement so that what followed had the quality of sensuous revelation.

Afterwards, they entered a little wooden hut on the

promenade. They changed out of their bathing costumes, removing their canvas slippers, peeling the sticky cloth of their bloomers down. They giggled with no idea of what entertained them.

'Liberation,' her cousin declared.

Ruth disappeared a year later into a premature death of which no one spoke or apparently knew the cause. But Grace remembered how she had uttered the word, their wet bodies shivering, their faces broadly smiling, and the sense of having discovered a new dimension of the world.

One quiet Sunday, a few weeks before the fire, she had walked in her undergarments into the lake at Ostrovo, anticipating enormous pleasure.

Two of the Australians, both accustomed to bathing and more comfortable romping half undressed, persuaded her to join them. When she entered the cool water a cloud of mosquitoes rose, and she panicked. She'd seen too many succumb to the fever of malaria and had resolved to stay well, and sane, and without tremors in her hands. She'd heard that locals burned dung and bathed upwind of the smoke, but this was offensive to her, and unenticing. The mosquito cloud was all motion and menace. It appeared to grow larger and move in a spotty mass towards her. The water was thick with mud and certainly unclean.

The sun blasted her head.

Olive and Stella stayed where they were, far from the shore, bouncing together like children and irresponsibly unafraid. They waved and called out. Grace could not hear what they shouted; her head was enveloped in insect hum. The cloud of living particles was the kind of disorder she most feared. She turned and retreated. She dragged her dripping body back up the slippery shore, covering herself and feeling defeated.

Later she heard rumour that the lake was full of dead Bulgars, pitched into watery graves from the campaign at Kaimakchalan. This confirmed her resolve not to swim in the lake.

There it was. From the entrance to the surgery tent she could see the strip of water radiant in the distance. She felt a pang, which she knew was a longing for Ruth, and for that day, and for sea-bathing in the Channel at Hastings. The sea-bathe retained its mythical aspect, a new-made body, ashine, and with the quake of an intimation. The sense of being held inside a larger organism.

Now the war, and now these damned mosquitoes.

Grace turned back to the tent to prepare. There had been a blast, and a Krupp gun, though it was just a skirmish by most accounts. She hated this language: 'skirmish', 'sideshow'. She hated 'sideshow' most of all; she had seen it in an English newspaper sent from home. 'Balkans Sideshow'. It meant they were less important and their efforts were worthless, with no real purpose, a form of entertainment. Still, a handful of seriously injured Serbs and French had been brought to her surgery. She watched the orderlies clean dirt from the begrimed soldiers, readying them for her instruments and her ministrations.

They'd all had enough, by now. Despite the bustle of preparation, they were already working with minds coarsened by repetition and fatigue.

Grace stood apart. Ceremoniously, she washed her hands with carbolic soap, wringing them as if demonstrating theatrical distress, but there was no distress, there was habit and distance. A young orderly, Agnes, shaved a soldier whose face had been destroyed and whose head gaped open. Grace watched as she manoeuvred the razor over the curves of his knobbly skull, pressing the ears gently forward, dabbing with a cloth, avoiding the wound. The man was semiconscious and might not yet know of his injury or defacement. His cheek was torn open, his left eye a pulp. He appeared to frown. Not the worst she had seen, but these elements gave her pause.

By now it was roasting hot. An unfamiliar bird

chirped its sharp notes above. It may have landed on the roof of the tent. The anaesthetist was ready, and the assisting nurse.

She noted that the soldier's left side was twitching, so that his fingers seemed restlessly to play finger exercises for piano.

Nerve damage, or brain injury, involuntary memory, or shell shock.

Grace stepped towards him. Now she entered her surgeon-mind, in which the body was interconnected systems of blood and guts. She listed to herself as she had when a student: *Frontal, parietal, occipital, temporal, cerebellum.* Then backwards: *Cerebellum, temporal, occipital, parietal, frontal.* In her mind's eye she saw the diagram with the lobes marked and named. This was an illustration that she had never forgotten: the brain perforated with lines, ready to be torn into neat sections.

From his uniform she knew that this man was a Serb, but it would be unwise at this stage to learn his name, or any details. She must itemise the injury. She must not consider the human factor.

In her work in the hospital in France, Grace had seen the conchies, the conscientious objectors, given the most degrading and menial of tasks, the cleaning of shit and vomit, burying severed limbs, or mopping spilled parts and fluids beneath the operating table. She saw men struggling with the gore of it, and with the effort to separate their work from their feelings. Here, there were no conchies, and the nurses and orderlies did everything.

She could exempt herself from the general duties. It was her skill and her status to deal with the technical problems, and she had the respect of the others for her calm efficiency. As long as she reminded herself of the strict order of anatomy, and the fact that there were measures—staunching, cutting, sawing, sewing—to retrieve a precarious life from mortal harm, then her role here had purpose and meaning. Duty, she told herself. All was duty.

Before the anaesthetic was given the man's left hand went still. His face was waxen. His frown disappeared. A nurse moved beside Grace and wiped her sweaty brow.

For a long minute she held her hand above the exposed brain, hesitating, waiting for a vital sign.

Mounds and channels, coral shape, the unperforated whole. Who would believe, seeing it, that consciousness resided there?

Grace no longer held any religious beliefs. There were no last things. There was no judgment or resurrection.

She did not believe a soul might exist and then leave, minuscule and coy, on diaphanous wings. Still, the moment spooked her; when soldiers died as she worked, she felt it as a personal slight and a professional failure. She had not even begun.

The old teachings were still there: 'For whosoever shall call upon the name of the Lord shall be saved'—Romans 10:13.

No saving here. No saviour. Those pitiable conchies. This orderly.

The orderly stared at her and then looked down. Poor Agnes Burden from Manchester, who would not meet her gaze, was now responsible for the cleaning-up. She began mopping furiously. Her face was averted and the rag in her hand was dark and sodden. Anguish: it was there in Agnes's expression. Grace had stronger defences but would not console or advise. Better the woman learned to cope.

It occurred to Grace that many of her patients frowned. Even very young faces, a man of only twenty or so, might display in his suffering an old man's frown. Something within them perhaps knew the idiocy of this war, of all wars, and of the waste that claimed them.

THERE WERE TIMES when Stella forgot why she was in Macedonia.

Swimming in the lake with Olive, writing jolly accounts in her diary.

There was no point in being sombre all the time. She believed in chin-up and perseverance. Some of her pieces, on the local customs of the region, had already been published in a newspaper in Australia. She had managed to convey how spirited the Allied troops were, how snobbish the French, and how gallant and chivalric the handsome Serbs. Their moustaches, she wrote, are truly magnificent, their muscles substantial. They have excellent teeth. They are like Sioux chieftains in their stance and physique, the consequence of wise eugenics.

In these pieces Stella was a *sestre*, a sister, not an incompetent cook and sometime orderly. She had signed an agreement of employment not to write of her time at the hospital, so wrote under a pseudonym. Her account wandered rapidly to the weather, and the locals, and the good-looking men. It was August 1917, but no mention was made of outrage at the war or demoralisation. She was a nationalist, and proud of it. She was an imperialist, and proud of it. She saw no contradiction in believing the British stock superior and the habits and customs of others quaintly amusing, but worthy of token respect. She called herself an 'Outlander', but was pleased to be among 'Homelanders'.

There was vanity, too. This was a contribution to the war effort, she told herself. Her being here, in Macedonia, pretending to be a cook, but all the while imagining a novel she might one day write about this adventure. It would be a romance between a *sestre* and a handsome Serb, and some derring-do, a love triangle (British captain, dashing but doomed), and perhaps a poignant death scene that involved an apple-cheeked grandmother sacrificed as she protected the hero and his love. They would part at the end, somehow tragically, just before their marriage, thus preserving the purity of their international union.

Stella had initially been assigned to the staff mess kitchen, superintended by a middle-aged woman called Stewart and three convalescing Serbs, Sreten, Zdravko and Yanko. She felt disrespected and unknown as an artist. Her battle was against the injustice to herself, not to take personally the position that paid no heed to her charm or humour or capacity to write. She was a short woman, overlooked, and for a time after she arrived, felt shorter. The kitchen arrangement made it possible for her to be a helper, not a cook, and in any case within a month she was made orderly to the matron, and dealt mostly with bed linen and the distribution of tobacco. She still did the rounds with tea, heaving the giant tin teapot; it allowed her out and about. But her self-assurance was shaky, and her purpose obscure.

This morning after the fire she woke to find her face a hive of mosquito bites. An orderly called May treated her with iodine solution. A lumpish woman from Lancashire, pasty and unblemished, May held Stella's chin between thumb and index finger and told her to stay still. The proximity was humiliating, to be seen so close up, to be encountered bitten even though, yes, she had definitely used the net, but no, she had not seen a tear or a gap. It was like a failure of some kind, to be the target of insects in the night. May leant the side of her hand against Stella's cheek as if she was painting a new detail on a portrait in oils. Stella looked upwards to the tent ceiling and the kerosene lamp hanging there. May was half her age, perhaps twenty, and acted like a boss.

'Quinine injection, next,' May said softly, in her singsong accent. And added a last poke of colour. 'There.'

May sat back, pleased, assessing her handiwork.

Stella resisted a huff. Later, she wrote in an article that she had been face-painted like a Maori or an Indian. She had become a primitive, she added. She was dotted with war paint in a torrid zone, endowed with a scary visage. It was the best she could come up with.

She lamented having no private mirror. A small hand mirror with a cracked ivory back was shared in her tent. In this oval she saw herself partially and in haste. What a fright: daubed. Reduced to mere surface and emptied of expression. How might she acknowledge herself, when her own reflection showed her so unlovely, all fault and stain. At least she still had her glory, her thick long hair, not cut in a bob like Olive or Grace. She had retained, she told herself, a precious femininity.

The attraction of Stella's work and location had begun to fade. From the beginning, she wanted more action. There was tedium behind the frontline and boring labour in the kitchen. Her work as factotum to the new matron was not much improvement. The patients' kitchen was busier, but that wasn't the solution either: she had imagined, though imprecisely, a heroic role for herself, some incident in which she alone was distinguished and brave. Matron wore a wound chevron of red cloth stitched high on her sleeve. Shrapnel, she'd heard. Somewhere near Liège.

Others at the hospital had served in France, and knowing nothing but propaganda Stella was envious of their labours. They had seen real action. She would lie awake on her stretcher, beneath her net, and without images or experience think *Action! Action!* as though zealous wishing would bring it near. One Australian soldier stationed with British troops told her of his grievous shame at inaction. He was willing to lose an arm or leg, he told her, to be out of this stinking, infested place. There were ANZACs who had survived Gallipoli only to be killed here, by mosquitoes.

On her afternoon off Stella enjoyed diverting swims or excursions to nearby villages, where she and other staff from the hospital bought souvenirs—a cowbell, a clay pot, coins women stitched onto their headdresses—and appreciated being treated as a novel presence. She looked forward to visiting Salonika again, now it was burnt. There might be tragedy to witness and the pathos of the refugee to describe. Her heart was full of righteous sympathy and the distinction of her book-learning meant that she might ennoble the city and honour it with her judicious witness. Olive had mentioned smouldering buildings and used the word 'catastrophic'. Stella would like to see 'catastrophic'. It would be something to write home about.

Nine months ago, before she arrived, there had been

terrible carnage, but this was a lull—everyone said so—a tedious lull. There were now rumours of Serbian Americans arriving in their thousands and well equipped to the north. There was talk of an impending Bulgar advance and Huns bringing in the gas. Here, arbitrary and inconsistent, it was Krupp guns and bomb blasts from time to time, and the usual medical problems of everyday life. One nurse, Elsie Fitzgibbon, had been discovered pregnant and sent back to Scotland. Stella was present when Elsie was lectured in front of a row of staff. She had offered no explanation, apology or excuse. Told of her sentence of repatriation, Elsie shrugged and scowled. All saw how she fiddled with her skirt, folding and refolding, but although they were captivated by her hectic fingers, none could decipher her meaning. A sly one, that Elsie.

Stella dreamt of this woman with something like envy. She'd not experienced sex, so she took the idea of it very seriously. The thought of pregnancy obsessed her and she wondered how Elsie Fitzgibbon had managed it, since their lives were so fundamentally constrained. Did she straddle a wounded soldier or take a Serb behind a tree? Was she forced, or had she taken advantage of a dying man, some naive, desperate fellow, wanting a woman's body to enclose his before the final disembodied darkness? There was guilty pleasure in inventing what might have happened, and a sense too of something more spiritually grave, new life here, in wartime, and the possibility of a joyful body.

Unbidden, shameful, 'Mademoiselle from Armentières' unrolled its jaunty verses in her head.

When injured soldiers were brought in, Stella felt excitement, wanting to witness damage, rather than malaria or dysentery. She might have been honourably concerned, but wasn't. She needed an assurance of the extremity of things, of a furnace that could consume them all. She needed a story. Her good cheer depended on it.

STANLEY FLICKED THROUGH his Bible. Ah, peace.

It was early evening. Around him, at their camp, soldiers were carousing, embracing, drinking local red wine and vomiting loudly into the bushes. He adjusted his spectacles and concentrated on the tiny script. The night was huge. His fingers were grubby. Carelessly, he left his thumbprint on a corner of the Psalms.

His family of eleven were Methodist and devout. Stanley had grown up convinced of the doctrines of his faith, nonconformity, resurrection, the eternal life of the spirit. No contrary evidence convinced him otherwise. No night of shelling and blasting. No bayoneted death. Nothing imperilled his certain heaven. When Stanley first arrived in Macedonia in June 1916, he was in time to see what and how soldiers might truly destroy. For most of the men the soul, any possible soul, was already tainted with trench slime.

Stanley raved on about the Light and the Lord, and his friend George listened with kind forbearance. Others paid not the slightest attention. That he was an artist made his mad loquacity explicable, but still an annoyance. The captain, a man of toad jowls and mauve protruding lips, whose amphibian appearance belied his fairness, counselled tolerance within the regiment. But Stanley must also shut up, he said. The British army couldn't abide a raver. For any cause whatsoever. Bolsheviks. Teetotallers. Even for God. The captain shook his jowls for emphasis and licked his lips a shiny purple. Gradually, Stanley learned to keep his opinions mostly to himself.

George was his only audience. When Stanley became agitated and needed the words he had spent a lifetime affirming, George listened, or at least pretended to listen, tilting his head to one side, like a dog paying attention. But he may have been dozing, or daydreaming, or off somewhere with the fairies. He may have been visiting his own memories. He'd told Stanley of two sisters who coddled him and fed him spoonfuls of bread soaked in warm milk. His father knocked him silly, but his sisters had been there to prop and to feed him.

On this first night after the Salonika firefighting, Stanley's devotions were interrupted by his arty imaginings. Angle, it was then. Refraction and skew were the new preoccupation. The human body seen from above or below, the rupture of perspective such as a tall mirror might provide, in which planes were reversed and images duplicated, or multiplied, or made distant and uncertain. In the field, he'd seen a vision of refraction. At Smol, four mule travoys brought wounded soldiers to a dressing station—an old

Greek church repurposed as an operating theatre—and now he imagined how, from above, this might look like a pattern of Providence: the stretchers fanning symmetrical before the doorway, the mules foreshortened but humbly leading, the light seeping from the church to illuminate their arrival. There would be able-bodied soldiers in the foreground and the casualties resting in simple shapes under dark blankets, the form of suffering, but not its essence. Essence was elsewhere, in light and alleviation.

Stanley's thinking was not clear, but the vision was. This painting would be produced in the future, in 1919. Without the reassurance of familiar things, he opted instinctively for those abstractions that made an objective correlative of his beliefs.

Mule travoys, moving towards light and healing: these compelled him to make sense.

And a small boy with an ikon, running away, stained red.

Stanley was very fond of mules. They were everywhere in Macedonia, perpetually working. Their fat heads enchanted him, their meek posture combined with their stolid, snorting labour. He liked their doggy smell and the thick must and dust that arose with a friendly slap. Sometimes they turned their heads slowly to nudge or inquire for a treat; he liked that too, that sense of timid communication.

So he had been given this task: to care for the regiment's six mules. After rain there was grass, but it had been a long, dry summer and the mules were now fed oats or sawdust to keep them going. Morning and evening Stanley watched as they perked up when he approached, then jostled, then pushed forward with their lowered heads, then snuffled and gobbled and lifted their scraggy necks for more. They were always hungry. Stanley named one of them Star, on account of what looked like his star-gazing, and this mule inspired particular affection. Star was a foreign mule. He'd been imported from Argentina. Spoke Spanish, Stanley joked. Danced the tango. Many mules died at sea and were pushed overboard, but Star had made it all the way to Macedonia to join the local animals in the service of war. In the illogic of the times, there was a new economy: populations of all sorts, humans and beasts, crisscrossing the globe so that men could line up to slaughter each other. Supplies of armaments, food, nurses, bullets. Star carried the raised slash of a jagged scar at his throat. Mules brayed at night, so those at the Front had their vocal cords removed. All agreed it was necessary for human safety. To Stanley—he couldn't prevent the association—it was like botched murder.

He placed his palm there and felt the hot throb of animal life.

George found him standing like this, with his palm at a mule's throat.

'Makin' a new friend? Sick of me, are you?' He smiled broadly. In the evening light the crevices of his wonky face made him look like one of the injured.

Stanley grinned in return, and felt relieved that George was half daft, and gentle. In the midst of so much that challenged him, this man did not. George tapped Star's head with a swift pat and handed Stanley a tin mug of tea, and they squatted together, away from the others, in the company of the tethered mules, which were heaving out their hot breath in unison, their flanks lightly touching, waiting among the human madness to resume their hard, silent work.

'Drink up.'

George was now playing mammy, or his sisters.

And Stanley recalled the boy running and wondered what kind of image this was, how it might be made meaningful separated out from Salonika, and the war. The stench of the world burning had stayed with him, in his hair and his clothes.

OLIVE SAW THE wound badge on the new matron's sleeve and wondered what had happened in Belgium. She'd been in Belgium and France with her ambulance, and they might have crossed paths. But there was a pact here that one didn't ask any questions. The Scottish Women's Hospital was a community of medical staff and volunteers who gathered in the field, then moved on. No one was encouraged to remember or talk of their service.

'No point remembering,' Matron said. 'Your work is before you, and now.'

She had auburn hair streaked with grey, and hazel eyes. She adjusted her uniform with a sharp tug and pointed with her chin to the tents. She was fifty or so, Olive judged, no-nonsense and tough. Her accent was Australian. Queenslander.

Matron had assembled her staff for the weekly summary on hospital matters. In the distance the lake glistened as a light breeze dimpled its surface. Despite the smoke, there was a brassy sky and Mount Kaimakchalan appeared to shine. 'Scotland of the East' some called this place, but the name didn't quite fit; the heat shifted surfaces, made vision and distance imprecise.

'No point remembering.' No talking cures here. No encouragement to spill your guts, as the Australians liked to say.

64

As if by sovereign act, Matron disqualified what haunted them, and what they held most dear.

There had been too much personal talk, she said. If a soldier or colleague wanted to confess, there was no duty to listen. Do not ask or prompt. Better left alone. For yourself, do not dwell on that which you have no power to control.

'No room for emotion,' she concluded. 'Duty.' This word sounded severe, left dangling like a noose.

Olive noticed Grace straighten her posture with dissent or assent. Hard to know. The surgeon stood at the front of the group and was looking down at her dusty boots. A brilliant physician, but remote. Some thought her a cold fish. Did she believe one should speak, or not, of the dark welter of images and feelings that the war brought with it? What composed their experience was surely not so easily dismissed as inconvenience.

Matron's words bounced concussive in her head.

It seemed another kind of duty, not to forget. Olive wanted to speak of what she had seen and known, though she suffered too much remembrance.

The heat was already high. Someone had left a plate of black grapes at the entrance of the mess tent—probably an offering from a grateful local—and they were now heated, abuzz with wasps and stinking sweetly. The staff were distracted by the buzzing grapes.

After her lecture on detachment, Matron briefed her team on the destruction of Salonika.

They had received no burns victims: ninety miles was too far to bring them. Other field hospitals had shouldered the load.

Congratulations to Olive for her sterling work.

Salonika, the burnt zone, was out of bounds for the time being.

Check the new rules on swabbing hands.

Bully beef and turnips again this week.

Dismissed.

With a sharp gesture, Matron summoned an orderly to remove the grapes. Then almost immediately there rose a savage howl. The young orderly had been stung on the cheek and fled in a panic, screaming. Another rushed off with her in a sisterly flurry, and Grace followed too, sedately. It fell to Olive to clear the mess. She again pulled on her mosquito gloves, seized the hot grapes and plunged them into a nearby bucket of water. Those wasps that did not drown climbed the side and around the rim, reeling like drunks before woozily they flew off.

Fucking wasps.

There were wasps as well as mosquitoes to deal with.

A snake or a scorpion visiting the tents led to the minor enthusiasm of an animal kill. There were half-wild dogs, which they struck with brooms and shovels. But for the most part, it was this ignominy, to be attacked by insects.

She was becoming nocturnal.

If she recalled Belgium or France, Olive stopped sleeping. There were entire nights when time and geography slipped away and she found herself falling backwards, so that bodies slid in and she revisited the worst of her memories. There was no volition or choice involved. She was at the mercy of these sudden slopes and, though she lay stiffly in the dark, clenched and careful not to call out, as the wounded often did in their own awful chorus, she was met by the voices and faces of the dying and the dead, by a scabby hand reaching up, or a broken collarbone, bloodied, jutting beneath a panting face, or some gap in a man's body that showed the gloss of his hurt flesh. She had seen men who looked bitten in half, as if mauled by metal teeth, and those so maddened and unaware they did not realise they were missing a hand or a foot. One man kept reaching for matches and ciggies in a hole in his body.

It astonished her how an event glimpsed for just seconds returned in such detail.

Olive listened in the dark to her own shallow breathing, sucking for air. She wiped her sweaty brow and remembered being caught in the shellfire, the thunder of the guns and the dirt falling over her sticky face, preparing her mentally for the first stages of burial. Men were shouting and grabbing their rifles.

Her chest tightened and banged. One night she thought she was having a heart attack.

Sometimes in the darkness Olive made herself rise. With her heart still thumping, she felt for her boots beneath the stretcher and slipped her sockless feet in, then lifted herself away from the slope. She drifted in silence past the mumbling and turning sleepers, towards the slim triangle of moonlight that was the opening to their tent. As she pulled aside the flap the whitish gap burst wider, and outside she saw how pearly and static the world had become, the other tents almost glowing, transformed to the flimsy cloth that might decorate a garden party or a wedding. Her body felt light and floaty; only her hands were heavy and hung loose and unfamiliar. There were rustlings somewhere, of grasses or small animals, and this was comforting, not disturbing, a sign of modest, hidden energies, leading their own shadowy lives. Around the encampment some of the tents shone faint yellow with nightshift duties, and she listened for the sound of soft talk or calling out.

At these moments it was self-possession she aimed for. Not to be overtaken, not to have the shakes. Not to believe her heart might rip open from an affliction of memory. She would press her heavy hands to her bosom wrapping firm, holding herself in.

On other nights Olive stayed put, mentally exercising. She countered her fearful self by dwelling on the difficulties of German grammar. Meeting dread with dread was how she thought of it. Her vocabulary was fine, her grammar appalling, so she rehearsed the cases, the genders and suffixes; she listed declensions, numbers and personal pronouns, though never entirely sure that she had the correct words or order. This practice brought her wild thoughts under control. The wave of tremor receded and she entered a reciting mind; the demand of correct usage, the age-old forms within language itself, seemed usefully to pacify and to hold her in place. That it was German practice was her own guilty secret. The language seemed to her sturdy as bricks and always building itself by accretion. A stonemason's language. An intellectual's language. The language too of *Lied,* in which Romanticism lived. And the surprising beauty of all these stern contradictions.

And tonight, in another slide, she saw again the grapes in the sun, the gift left by strangers at the entrance to the mess tent. There was a goat's head once, left for stew or soup. It stared at the nurses with fat, glaucous eyes. There was a sole pomegranate and a plate of spiced oily olives. And recently, last week, a pyramid of perfect lemons.

GRACE WAS INTRIGUED by the new matron's command to forget. She looked down at her feet, then up again at Matron's round, vacant face, and thought it an ignorant command that severed the mind and body. Matron knew nothing of advances in understanding the dynamic qualities of the mind. An Australian, unlettered. A pudgy, ugly woman. Grace considered all Australians essentially ignorant.

A year ago, on leave from France, she'd read Brill's translation of Sigmund Freud's *The Interpretation of Dreams*. This was science at last, not hocus-pocus. She was convinced of the artful ingenuity of mental processes, and loved the dreams Freud described and his forms of explanation. There were manifest and latent meanings in everything, she concluded, not only dreams. This had been a revelation. And the rest: infant intensity, wish fulfilment, unspeakable desires, ruthless parents. All of it thrilling. Freud knew the laws of correlation and the motivating power of sexual need. He took the inner life seriously. He discussed himself and his patients in a manner so candid and explicit that from time to time Grace needed to pause her reading and place the book facedown before her.

The hottest time, in the middle of day, was when

everyone wrote letters. After the fluster of wasps and the general bustle of disquiet, the staff had been dismissed to their two hours of midday rest. Grace sat perched on her stretcher and wrote to her brother Gerald. Temporarily released from the Somme, he was now at the Craiglockhart Hospital near Edinburgh, where he wore a blue armband that told everyone he was an officer. He sent her accounts of the long, dreary corridors and the humourless physicians, of the wheelchairs, the gardens and the sloping lawns. Of the lines of mutilated men placed in weak sunshine to revive and encourage them. Bluntly, he described how his roommate Barker rose at night and wandered in a small circle, checking a rifle that wasn't there, looking through a trench periscope that wasn't there, recoiling in a dramatic flinch when he heard the blast of a non-existent bomb. He crouched in the centre of the room, waiting for the assault in his mind to be over. He crouched for so long that he fell asleep in the posture of a man assaulted. It was exhausting just to witness it, night after night, this particular delusion, this sullen isolation. Gerald had asked to be moved to another room, but was refused.

'We're all mental here,' he wrote. 'Mental as anything.'

In his most recent letter Gerald mentioned that the Freud book she'd sent him a year ago remained unread.

He wasn't up to it, really, though it would have been handy in this place. Psycho-somethings, most of them, the treating physicians. They ask your dreams, he wrote, and believe in the retrieval of memories. 'I try to oblige, eccentrically.'

The siblings adopted a slightly wry tone in their letters—he mindful of the censors, she of upsetting him—confiding but not wholly, cynical but tempered, each eager to impress the other with some curious or entertaining snippet.

The local band had that morning regaled patients with a chipper version of 'The Teddy Bears' Picnic' and it had been amusing to nod off in the sunshine, Gerald wrote, like a spoilt child or an old codger. On waking he had been ordered to play badminton for his jumpy nerves. Every day he saw men with eyes swollen from crying and electrical treatments.

'We pretend jollity,' he continued, 'in our neuro-degeneration. Oh Grace, what to say? Tea and scones (only for officers) are incompatible with trembling and shame.'

In her reply Grace sent a foolishly guarded letter. *Tip-top! Keep your chin up!* How she wished later she had scratched out that particular inanity. She wanted to tell Gerald of

David, the amputee, whom she had murdered. And of the man with the head wound whose hand had suddenly stopped twitching. But soldiers' death stories would not help a shattered brother, electrocuted and abject and obliged to play badminton. Instead, she wrote in comic tones about the mosquitoes that oppressed them, and of how this was considered a time of lull in the fighting.

Might lull be connected to lullaby? she asked.

The absence of books here was a terrible deprivation.

And Salonika: Grace wrote to Gerald once again of Salonika. Such a fascinating city. It had been a delight to hear Ladino and French, Italian and Greek, Turkish and Serbian, all in the same space. The Allied Army of the Orient brought regiments from all over, so she'd seen soldiers from the protectorates, Senegal and Annam, others from India, Russia, as well as France and Britain. The Senegalese, she wrote, were beautiful men, ebony and shining. She had never seen a black man up close before. *Tirailleurs*, they were called. She had not known that black skin carried such attractive light.

Now she wondered where all these soldiers were. Back in camp, no doubt, or returned to the Front.

Grace wanted to revisit Salonika, to see what was left. Olive had described buildings falling in a pile of sparks in the street, and the destruction of monuments and holy places. The shopping area was gone, she said, and the Café Cristal. But Grace could not tell her brother that Salonika had been destroyed. And if he read of it later in the *Scotsman*, he would probably not let on. She preserved the city unburnt in her head, just as she had, for a short while, preserved David by not attending to his death.

She wanted to write: I am troubled not only by David, but also by his companion, a man who sobbed and ran his hand like a plough through his hair. As he fled, wholly stricken, I did nothing to respect him, as if his breaking open of true feeling embarrassed and offended me.

He reminded me of you, darling Gerald. The companion reminded me of you.

Instead, she wrote: *I miss English mizzle, all that cool, damp air and the blue tint to children's faces and the softened outlines of brown houses. The way wool is matted and glistening with almost invisible rain. The way the droplets are uniform, in a pattern, and align like anatomy their miniature designs. Do you know, darling Gerald, the etymology of mizzle?*

And she wanted to describe a dream. When the war was over she would tell Gerald that the very night of David's death, the night of the fire in the city of Salonika, she dreamt that his companion had rushed towards her with his rifle upraised. The bayonet was fixed. She expected blame and violence. But the companion did not act. He drew to a halt, braced like a tin soldier, and saluted her with a creaky mechanical jerk. Somehow this show of army discipline, this man become toy, was more terrifying.

When the war was over she might send this dream to Dr Freud. He was a fellow physician. He would understand the pressure of surgery and the guilt of mistakes. She would confide to him that in her dream she was wearing a Sam Browne belt. She had a pistol tucked away, hidden under her arm, nestling warm and secure and comforting, near her breast.

TENTATIVE WORLD, SHE had called it; this mere cloth that housed and leant over them.

Like the others, Stella was resting on her stretcher. The heat outside was formidable, but inside it was smothering. Furtively, she checked her mosquito bites in the hand mirror. They were less inflamed, but brown iodine still spotted her face. She bent her head, peered, and noted the defacement in her diary. She made it sound worse than it was. Not so much a book of remembering, she reflected, as of colourful reconstruction.

It was her habit at rest time to write as much as possible, and this led to errors with spelling and grammar, and a loose direction to her scribbled narrative. She wrote descriptions of the scenery, and dwelt again on the brave Serbs and their magnificent moustaches. She wanted to write of Elsie Fitzgibbon's disgrace, which so obsessed her, but this could perhaps be regarded as unfair, or indecent. One of the nurses suggested that Elsie could have taken Dr Lawson's Cure for Blockages, but there were no such potions in a field hospital in Macedonia. No women's medicines. They made do and sometimes it wasn't enough. Elsie Fitzgibbon had enraged Matron and excited the others because she seemed to have no regrets. She'd been almost three years with the Scottish Women's Hospital and perhaps, sick of the war, wanted a future elsewhere. She was private and superior with her secret experience.

Had she been inclined, Stella might have tossed off a patriotic verse or two for the papers back home. *Oh Glorious Scots Women, Savers of Empire's Sons!*

Easy: she knew the rhetoric, she knew all the rhymes. But she was bored and hot. She saw the industry of others writing their dutiful letters and wondered why she had so little energy only to connect.

One of the nurses nearby was stitching her hem, bending over a small tear in her dress.

Suffragist: Hilda Macdonald.

Stella wanted the approval of the Scottish suffragettes. They were admirably confident and in their company she believed herself smarter. Most were better educated than she and spoke foreign languages. Hilda looked up gravely, surfacing from the inward work of her own thoughts as she stitched, and, catching Stella's gaze, offered a kindly smile. Stella nodded, suddenly shy. They were a community wholly of women, but the patients were men. This was the basis for Stella's noble sentiments, but also the ground of her keen sense of exclusion: that she was not a nurse, but ran errands, that she did not handle the bodies of men, disempowered, pitiable, exposed in their woundings, but stood nearby holding bandages or a giant tin teapot. Once she had been called on to lather faces for a shave: this was her only recollection of touching the men, holding a finger at their chins as she wiped the foam downwards and along their cheeks. Every man had averted his eyes.

There was some kind of kerfuffle outside and each woman in the tent became still. A ripple of fear slid among them as they heard a lorry approach. Hilda was already rising. Unexpected visitors were grinding up the road; the clanking of gears and the straining wheeze of the vehicle grew closer. There was a rough grumble as the lorry pulled to a halt. Hilda peeled back the tent flap and peeped out.

'One of ours.'

And then they all rose to see what novelty had arrived.

Their rest time had been broken by the arrival of a lorry full of frozen rabbits. Australian supporters of Serbia had sent fifty thousand carcasses to be distributed at the Eastern Front. Two Australian soldiers were charged with the task. The diggers looked eighteen or so, pleased with the reception they received at each camp, as the bringers of meat. Meat! One rushed up to a pretty nurse, grabbed her hand and shook it. He expected to be congratulated, but she flinched at his meaty smell and facetious manner. She withdrew her hand, but he seemed not to notice. They were in high spirits, these boys: who could blame them?

The hospital share was unloaded. One crate was opened so that staff could assemble and marvel at the gift.

'Good heavens!' It was Matron. 'Just the ticket!'

The rabbits were all without heads and skinned. Some had been misshapen by freezing, so that they looked agonised and twisted. Their greyish bodies were veined with white threads of sinew, their forelegs extended in a parody of running away. It would be a huge task to cook them. Rabbit stew forever. In a letter from home Stella had read of the rabbit-catching for the Front—threepence for a small one, sixpence for a large, *money for bunnies*— and here they were, hard little packages stacked in crates. There was a message scrawled in red paint: *With Greetings from Melbourne, Victoria.*

Inside, the lorry was muggy with condensation and carried the reek of drains. There were blocks of ice wrapped in hessian, already melting.

Zdravko and Yanko helped the soldiers unload. They were taller than the Australians and seemed to take control; they were grinning and joking, vastly amused, as they lifted the crates from the lorry. There were local rabbits and hares, but they'd never seen such abundance, an entire vehicle stuffed to the roof and with greetings from Melbourne, Victoria.

No refrigeration, Stella was thinking, no bloody ice. How would they manage? She'd opened cans of rabbit meat, hundreds of them, but this was a new challenge.

Matron appeared at her side to command Stella to bring tea to the visitors. Hilda Macdonald had heard, she was sure, and she felt a torment of humiliation that she was publicly designated tea lady. Knowing they'd all performed menial chores didn't help; she wanted to show her intelligence and competence, her suitability to the war effort. She'd been here only two months and was still trying to make herself known as *herself*. She hurried off to lift the teapot from the fire and returned to serve the two young soldiers their over-stewed tea. Neither acknowledged her. Both took extra sugar, when there were rations to observe. Then they were on their way.

Stella was summoned back to their mess kitchen to help with the preparation of the rabbits. There they were, a wall of crates of frozen carcasses: she felt the cool of them and smelt the metallic whiff of early thawing. If this heat continued, there would soon be a wall of rot and muck.

There were too many; they should donate a portion of the frozen rabbits to those in the village, or further away, in the refugee camp. At the wooden plank that served as their table, Stella chopped a few onions and used the last of their potatoes. Zdravko contributed a kind of garlic jelly, the slimy grey of snail trail, which revolted her. Stewart decided this paste would be kept separate and reserved for the Serbian patients; no point upsetting their own.

'*Kouneli stifado!*' Zdravko insisted, but they were all afraid of traditional rabbit stew that might contain such stuff. Zdravko muttered something that indicated the depth of their offence.

As the rabbits thawed, Stewart added, some would be salted for preservation. Stella had no idea how this was done. And they would need to find salt.

The wall of meat incited a memory of Stella's father. His smeared hands were pulling the skin off a still-warm rabbit, speedy and efficient, as if removing a furred glove. He held the skin before her, dangling, then flicked it in her direction and told her to hang it on the wire fence to dry in the sun. When he sliced open the carcass, there were half-a-dozen little rabbits inside, curled lolly pink and neat, their eyes sealed as if sleeping.

THE SLANT OF shadow on a face, the crosshatching that made it curve.

Stanley stood slowly and extinguished his Woodbine with the heel of his boot. He was sketching his regiment at rest, smoking, playing cards, lounging around. He had no interest in depicting the various atrocities of combat but saw here a kind of community, a group of men mostly getting along, with no rebellion in the ranks but a general brotherhood and shared purpose. He may have idealised.

He leant his pencil sideways and shaded the face of a man he admired, Granville, one of the quiet ones, but brave, and in his third year at war. Henry Granville had been repatriated after the Battle of Doiran, all nerves and tics, and with a belly full of shrapnel, but then, surprise, surprise, he rejoined the regiment. Others felt ambivalent about his return. They claimed he had changed, turned inward more often, but he said in his own defence that he 'was none the worse for wear'. Most felt he was a stranger moving among them. Possibly what they saw was a man who had been freed, but then chose to return to the prison of the war. There was this broader context, in which they were moved around, singly or in groups, according to mass forces of strategy they could only guess at. They were bound to this, this bigger plan, which held their lives tight. No one talked of the future anymore.

Granville had a nervous habit of patting his moustache; he kept straightening his uniform; he was startled by sudden sounds. He brought them a tin of shortbread biscuits from home, and they had stood in a circle, each taking one, each feeling self-conscious and greedy at this secular communion. Stanley understood that Granville represented what they most feared: random injury, random recovery, then to find oneself back where one started, with no end in sight. The nightmare of repetition.

They asked him about Home. He said that pubs were still pubs, a pint was still a pint, but that women were driving buses and working in factories. There were bombings in London and Devon and further north. Zeppelins slid at night above the cities and left ruination in their wake.

A few were impressed by 'ruination'. He was a reader, Granville, and knew a thing or two about how to conceal the bloody mess they were all caught in, types of violence that didn't have a name at all. Most had heard of the bombings from weeks-old newspapers, but 'ruination' didn't quite fit. One of the privates, Marshall, said he'd lost a sister and her two children just a mile from St Pauls in a night-time raid. Marshall sneered at 'ruination'. It insulted his sister and her babes. They saw that he would have liked to smash Granville's face but saw too that the urge passed almost as soon as it arrived and he sank back into himself and his hatred of the frigging ponce Granville, who had no right to return.

It made things grimmer, knowing that the war had spilled over the Channel.

Stanley was proud of his portraits. And most soldiers were pleased to be drawn, finding a second self there, in this odd man's feathery lines. He was good, give him that; they recognised themselves and others and saw something in his compositions that looked right, as if there was a way of seeing that ennobled their presence. Stanley worked briskly and then gave away his sketches. He would keep nothing of his time in the regiment, only visiting later, by memory, that which comprised his visual war. For now it was these men, bringing them into focus, making the best likeness he could manage. Away from the Front they were in possession of ordinary humanity. It was a charm, to show them again full and, for the time being, safe.

He'd sketched George many times. George sent a couple of the portraits to his sisters: proof of life and a need to return, if only as an image. And for Stanley too this was a satisfaction: George was in awe of his skill and had assumed a role as his protector. He was a big man and

Stanley was reedy and thin, with the body of a boy; all his life he had attracted spiteful surmise. He was afraid of Marshall, in particular, who had a temper and a head stuffed with rage and loss; he would need little provocation to skewer a man with his blade or crush another's life with his chubby bare hands.

Crossing the clearing, Stanley joined the company of his mules. It was what he did, use mule care as an excuse to enter his own animal thoughts. Not feathery surface and planar, but a deep-down inside. The mules shuffled and snorted as he approached, bowed their long heads, seemed to sweat and to sigh as men did in the throes of malaria. By now he had named them all, but Star was still the favourite. Stanley touched his quivering flank, hooked two fingers in the metal loop of the bridle, and leant his cheek there, sentimental, sure of the purity of his wonder at these parallel lives. He could hear Star's heart, da-boom, da-boom, and the regular pump and swish of his blood. The hide was prickly, like grass, animal and vegetable together. But docile, unwarlike. Stanley nudged with his face.

'So here you are.' It was the captain. Stanley sprang back. Saluted. 'This is what you get up to.'

Stanley stood at attention, waiting for a reprimand or a slight.

Captain began a little speech about how each soldier has a role to play. There was no shame in being caught at the Eastern Front at a time of lull. There was no shame in tending the animals that served the British Empire.

Stanley was confounded: he'd never felt any shame in tending animals.

Captain went on: 'But you have other gifts. I have seen the sketches.' He paused, waiting for Stanley to divine his meaning. The pause went on too long.

'I would like you to sketch me,' the captain said, careful not to sound vain or imperative. But he must not concede any want or imply subordination.

The day was hot and bright. Above them flitted a handful of red-tailed scrub robin. There were wild raspberries here and in good times the locals cultivated grapes and olives. In another life Captain might have been Alexander the Great. There might have been a band of merry men and plenty to eat.

Now Captain looked wary and vaguely imploring.

But it was quickly settled. Word spread that Stanley was to draw a portrait of the captain. That he had such distinctive features pleased Stanley enormously: the moist puffy eyes, the jowls, the mauve-toned complexion; he was a man verging, like himself, into the realm of wildlife, already transmogrifying. The men studied each other. It was Captain who turned away first, superstitious perhaps, or not wishing to be inspected outside the boundaries of love or art. He leant over to make a show of patting a mule. His gesture was awkward and his affection unconvincing.

'And no raving!' he added. 'The army will not abide a raver.'

Stanley was still rigid, standing at attention. He was thinking that he wanted to befriend Henry Granville. It was Granville, not the captain, whose good opinion he sought. The man who had left, and then, reconstructed, returned.

AT THE CENTRE of Salonika, when it was still intact, a London bobby directed traffic from a little stand at the end of Venizelos Street, at an intersection the Britishers liked to call Piccadilly. He wore a long jacket, high hat and impeccable white gloves, and stood waving and flapping his hands, gesturing, beckoning, ushering cars forward, halting bigger vehicles for a frisky pony trap, allowing the slow progress of a wooden cart drawn by a mule, guiding the pedestrians, the stragglers, those pulling heavy hand-carts. He wore MP on his sleeve, but he was still a bobby. On the French map Olive possessed it was rue Vénizélos which ran into rue Egnatia, the *Via Ignatia*, the ancient road stretching all the way to Constantinople. She was delighted by the layers and complications of names, and by the unreality of the London bobby, performing his hand puppetry in the pretence of keeping everyone safe.

In France the Tommy soldiers had named their trenches: Piccadilly, Marble Arch, Tottenham Court Road. One man she loaded into her ambulance had said he 'copped it at Covent Garden' and she thought that he was simply delirious with pain. The place names made London omnipresent to them, a dismal map-in-the-head that guided nothing, signified nothing, but reminded them of a distant, solid ideal. When later she heard the details of the battle it seemed the least of the madness, to want to vouchsafe a city centre still imagined as inviolable. To be safely entrenched. To assert grid and location. The same soldier had grabbed at her arm with a fierce grasp and whispered, 'I can feel cold at the bottom of my brain.' Olive had wiped his damp forehead and replied too cheerily, 'We'll soon warm you up!'

She had not meant to be callous.

Olive was on leave when she saw the bombing of London. With her sister, Violet, and brother-in-law, Alfred, she'd been on a night out to the Duke of York's Theatre in the West End. *Romance* was an American drama about a pure clergyman falling for a sinful opera singer. Olive thought it soppy and ridiculous, but secretly enjoyed the flowery speeches and the wild proclamations of love. Madame Cavallini, the opera singer, wore a crown of feathers and multiple necklaces and was the apparition of a glamour they could barely remember. She swept around the stage in a white velvet dress, fanning her painted face, turning to the audience directly when she revealed her history as a mistress. It was a tragic story, but in the satisfactory way of love, not war. Violet adored it and wept at the end, shielding her face with her hanky. Alfred sniffed to show he was unaffected and helped them into their coats, although the September evening was clement and mild.

They left with the crowd in bouncy theatre-bustle and it was a sound, first of all, that quieted and stilled them. Olive heard a loud doo-da, doo-da, doo-da, doo-da, as if there was a pulse in the sky, a breathing apparatus of some kind, beating a steady rhythm. Above them it swung into view, high and silver as moonlight. The mythical zeppelin drew everyone's gaze. It was irresistible. There was incomprehension, then a racing comprehension of danger; the crowds in the street, coming from the theatre, began to run for shelter. The drumming rumble grew louder but the form itself was calm and remote, the glow of its belly unearthly as a chrysalis. In physical proportion it was impossible to calculate, but even as they ran they looked up, to see something so extraordinary, to be able to say, 'Yes, I saw it, I saw the zeppelin.'

Violet, like many others, believed that they were piloted by women.

The plan had been to take the Charing Cross tube home, but Alfred, excited, commanded a taxi. They piled in and Olive realised soon enough that this was not an escape, but an impulse to follow the trail of the airship. Alfred took control and the excited driver was keen to obey. They followed as it sailed and scintillated and drifted; they watched as it dropped the first heavy cargo of bombs.

They were on Shaftesbury Avenue heading north when a spray of fire burst ahead of them. Alfred shouted, 'Go! Go!' and the driver, confused, veered away before he realised he was meant to move closer. Violet was huddling in the dark; Olive was watching with a mixture of alarm and fascination, the world turning as the driver pulled at the wheel, Alfred, his face to the glass, his manner boyish and stupid, and the zeppelin ballooning too close now, so that she feared they'd slide beneath it. London shops rushed by, and the shapes of running citizens. A bus was on fire, and there must have been people inside, but casualties were invisible in billow and speed. Only one or two men ran towards the bus—it stood aglow, strangely isolated, under a column of black smoke. A sign reading Gilbey's Invalid Port lay to one side, blown off and separately burning.

There was petrol stink and blackness streaming in the air. Air-raid sirens whined high and ineffectual.

London was remapping itself around her, as the zeppelin led them further north into a tunnel of fires. Olive was not sure where they were: taller buildings, lit in flashes; the swoop of a corner around a dark park with a fountain at its centre; houses, not shops. Ornate pilasters loomed up, then fell away. Alfred was at last seized by rational fear and ordered the taxi driver to take them home. Now he pounded at the glass behind which the driver's plaid cap bobbed. He was shouting, 'Turn round! Turn round, I say!' and fell back breathless into the stifling darkness. He took Violet into his arms, but she was already distraught and furious, unforgiving of his frenzy.

'We'd better be getting back,' Olive said firmly. To support him, to criticise him, to assure the driver they'd had enough amusement for one night.

This was a dim and fearful London. The streetlamps were out and windows were covered with cardboard and blackout curtains. Families were already crouching together, the wealthy in their cellars, uncomfortably cooped with their servants.

Olive knew the lake at St James's Park had been drained so that zeppelins could not use its black-mirror reflection to locate the palace at night.

She imagined the headlines: *Home Front Assaulted!* And a grainy photograph of a woman standing forlornly beside a pile of bricks that had been a house, or Home Front ambulance men carrying a body on a stretcher under the distress signal of a white sheet.

Nothing like the trenches, of course. She knew what a trench looked like.

When they arrived at Kensal Green she saw that the taxi driver, a man in his sixties and too old to enlist, had the same flush of eagerness as young recruits seeing their first flares and action at a distance. He touched his cap in gratitude for the special fare. His hands were shaking, his eyes were bright. Alfred held his arm around Violet and was ushering her up the front steps when a maid with frightened eyes opened the door and let them in.

Olive despised them all, and herself, for being safe and sound.

She thought of the drama of Madame Cavallini, and despised that too, and then of Gilbey's Invalid Port, in which she might have drowned her sorrows. She thought of the airship and its undulant, silver sweep over their heads, its doo-da, doo-da, doo-da, doo-da, its manifestation. In her bed she tried to arrange these matters in a human order, but a thick, quiet darkness had fallen around her, the raid over now and the excitement abated, so that she stopped trying to make sense and bring her feelings under control, she stopped the turn and return of the images of the night, and as if she was on a slow rocking train let herself be carried away—a tunnel of black this time, a pacification—and she slept the deep, dreamless sleep of those divinely forgiven, so that the maid had to give her a little shake to rouse her in the morning.

Ah, she had slept.

What was the difference? The difference was that she had seen no bodies.

LOCALS CALLED IT *ta kammena*, the burnt zone. Salonika the burnt.

Small fires were yet to be extinguished. The cellars would smoulder and reek for months. The air was corrupted. Grace searched for a building she recognised but saw only pall and debris and the smoke of a world gone.

From somewhere she heard an American song: *You made me love you, I didn't wanna do it...* A woman's voice, plaintive, accompanied by piano.

It was the third day after the fire and Grace was in Salonika to check what was left of medical stores. Olive had driven her along the Monastir road, which was partially clear, so they'd made good time. Both were silent for most of the journey. As the lorry approached the burnt zone, they began to cough with shared nervousness or the inhalation of disaster. Grace asked to be dropped off near the centre and to meet in an hour at the quay. They would deal with business later. She wanted to walk alone through the burnt metropolis, to see for herself what the city looked like. It would take a little time before she understood her own motives.

Grace found herself not far from the old agora and the Roman forum, both blackened but standing. Stones persist, she thought. Stones.

The song again; it must have been playing from a gramophone: *And all the time you knew it, I guess you always knew it...*

She was heading towards the sea, through ruins, trailed by a melody.

Before her all was recomposed as fallen shapes, and the warm breeze of late August was dense with black dust. All ruination, she thought, but for the preserved modern song, a discrepancy which struck her as somehow typical of wartime. She looked around but couldn't locate the source of the music. It was surely miraculous, a gramophone playing a song in this demolished place. Someone had retrieved it, dusted it, set the record on the turntable.

Groups of men were shovelling bricks and char. Others distributed flatbread from the back of a bullock cart to a clutch of citizens who remained. From a water tank, figures in uniform filled tin cans and buckets, to be borne away on the heads of sorrowing women dressed in striped skirts. There were idle soldiers, French and British, on who knew what duty, standing around, irritated and bored, charged ignominiously with guarding something they believed to be worthless.

A little boy was pestering them, offering a miniature

ikon for sale. One of the Tommies raised a rifle and pretended to shoot him.

Bang! and a make-believe jolt of recoil.

The boy danced backwards, taunting. When he approached Grace she was appalled by how dirty he was, his clothes stained red, his face scaly with filth or rash. He had a harelip that made her wonder if he was an orphan and rejected. Aware of her gaze, the boy gestured hunger, touching his mouth. In his hand she saw the image of Demetrius, the patron saint of Salonika, depicted as the warrior martyr. The morose-looking saint wore Roman armour and carried both sword and spear. It was a singed, unholy image, more than likely a picture card pasted onto wood, but she took it anyway and gave the boy a few coins in return. He paused for a moment, surly, as though he expected more, but then he whooped a little whoop, held up his fist with the money, and sped away. She'd been an easy touch, she guessed, but could not have refused such a piteous appeal.

Unlike Olive, Grace had never seen the Front. She'd worked long hours over bodies shot and blasted towards their deaths, but the field hospitals were at a distance from the killing and the bombed-out cities. She was not even conscious of the thought—that Salonika might substitute, that this city might show what mass tragedy was—but it was there inside her as a shapeless, inexplicable longing, wicked in a way, and possibly unconscionable. She could not deny she wished to see a city destroyed, a great and awful unmaking.

Alla-hu-Akbar!

A thread of muezzin vowels from afar. What she'd once thought sonorous and lovely, Grace now heard as a wail.

A woman, her head covered and her expression obscure, approached on the street. With both hands she was clutching a single aubergine to her chest. In the past, at medical school, Grace had been told she 'looked Jewish'. It was meant as an insult. This woman looked Jewish and seemed to carry Grace's face. But there was no nod, no recognition, even though Grace saw the startling likeness and felt disposed to offer fellow feeling and a sign of her interest and care.

'Hallo.' It was a woeful attempt at fellowship. *'Bonjour?'*

Grace stood still, tense and doubtful. This was one of the few moments in her life she would recall as a possible phantasm. As a kind of yearning made real. An effect of amazement.

But the woman did not respond and showed no sign of having heard her greeting. She passed Grace without a glance and did not look back. There was possibly no other woman walking alone in the old town and Grace felt dispirited, almost insulted, not to have been seen. She was invisible to this woman who was so visible to her. Her foreignness had both disguised and unsexed her.

So, it may have been an encounter that she was seeking. Not the filthy boy, skipping away in a feeble, private triumph; not a substituted vision to give expression to unnameable feelings of ruin; but a woman, out of the blue, who uncannily resembled her. The attachment was to herself. Or to another self.

The call to prayer had ceased, the American song was behind her, and the streets were quiet but for the business of cleaning up. There were very few lorries or cars, and those were mostly on the big roads. Here too work groups were organising clear and sift, and the ambient sound was of the rough scrape and drag of shovels. There were no women's voices. Now and then a command or a shout rose from the debris. Most of the ruins were still too hot to remove or search. Fires persisted in nooks and crannies; even a few bigger buildings thought saved were newly igniting. Looking at her boots, Grace was aware of loose ash underfoot. She thought: *Be careful, do not slip.* Her knowledge of injury was activated at such times: a doctor's bleak mindfulness.

Ahead lay the shells of two cars. They appeared as if crouched and self-protecting. Perhaps when they cooled children would sit in them and pretend to drive. Perhaps the cars would be claimed for scrap metal and refashioned into small, useful objects. Grace had no idea of the stages of recovery a city might go through, or why she stood gazing blankly, paused, at two bent empty shapes.

And the sea, the Aegean. At the far end of the street the sea was visible as a pool of gold light, a residual permanency beyond the impermanent shapes of the city. This served the purpose of a mirage in a desert, a hazy vision to pull the lost drifter forward. The sun made a bright aisle to lead her there.

At the corner, she stopped. Tried to get her bearings. What had once been a pharmacy was now a mass of fused glass. There was a black mound of burnt wood, with glitter at its centre. Bottles of lotions and potions had melted to a cake of vitreous shine, reverting from shape to formless substance. Grace pushed at the mass with her boot; a crust had already solidified. It was a new, unrepeatable object made in the furnace of the blaze.

She roused herself, moved forward. The streets were wider now. Everything more spacious. Across rue Egnatia lay the remains of a confectionary store. Grace smelt the seared sugar, acrid and sharp, before she understood the location and realised that it was a place she had visited before. Sweets had been sold there only last week, stacked in neat cardboard boxes and tied with satin ribbon. The window display of the store was legendary: ziggurats and mountains of Turkish delight, pastry squares made of pistachio and honey, almonds coated in sweet shells and arranged in gift bags of voile. She'd loved this place, its decadence, and the scent of what had been strictly forbidden to her as a child. But, like the glass in the pharmacy, the sugar had heated and oozed into organic shapes. It had hardened into a pavement of dark toffee.

She knew that most of the destroyed shapes in the streets were old houses. Gone now but for thicker beams in a ravaged crisscross. This was an added confusion. Rectangles of stone showed the former foundations. Damp piles of belongings were stacked in the street, but there was little evidence otherwise of domestic life.

Grace came across a smashed mirror, perhaps dropped in an instant of terror. It flashed at her, lively, as she stepped on the facets of its face.

~

Thousands had lost their homes and those things that matter, an ornament, a keepsake, a photograph, a cat. Some people had been burned and some people had died. In the ferocious measurements of wartime, the numbers were considered small. This was it: proportion, percentage, the way a war or a firestorm might shift relations from the single to the mass, from the individual face to deplorable graphs and crass generalisations. The Allies had expected the Bulgars to take advantage, to bomb or attack in the sorry aftermath; but the enemy had refused their advantage and stayed away. Why, she wondered. Our side would have acted. Our side would have advanced to make a slaughterhouse among the ruins.

She felt a need for coffee, strong Turkish coffee.

An awareness of her own dying, or capacity to die, had come to her, moving through the burnt-out city.

But she also felt a new vigour. She was thirty-four years old and her, life was still ahead of her. At some point in the future, in a smart, new café in a rebuilt Salonika, she would sit with Gerald and describe all she had seen in the summer of 1917. They would drink coffee served in engraved glasses by a tall man dressed in a red bolero and fez. She would describe the black chaos and melted shapes that stank of chemicals and sugar. She would mention the boy with the ikon, the Jewish woman with the aubergine, and the song, the torch song, sexual and lamenting, which continued to play in her mind. In this future projection, it was peacetime. Rebuilt Salonika was magnificent.

AT THE FIELD hospital the mood had settled after the excitement of the rabbits. The tents all stank faintly of meat thawing, but good sense had prevailed and some carcasses had been donated before they spoiled. Stella watched grateful women stash dead rabbits into woven baskets lined with straw. They slung them over their backs and walked off towards the mountain. A few crates had been given to the small town of Vodena—men arrived with two covered mule carts, clearly expecting many more, but were politely thankful. She saw how carefully they disguised their disappointment, not wishing to be shamed, not wishing to admit hunger.

Greetings from Melbourne, Victoria.

Stella was showing the beginnings of fever. She had been fortified by rabbit stew—real meat at last—but was direly afraid of the quinine injection. The dread was entirely rational: nurses called it 'the bayonet charge'. It was a long needle, about two and a half inches, too long to imagine entering the soft surface of a human body.

She wondered what a 'heart murmur' was and imagined she might have one as she stood in the sticky heat, agitated, waiting, her heart fast with fear. The nurse they called Smithy turned to prepare the injection.

There was the tiny clink of metal instruments lifted

and returned to a tray and the decisive snap of a glass ampoule.

Stella watched Smithy's hips move at her task, but then looked away, at anything, really, the peak of the tent, the hanging lamp in its metal case, the fall of wavery light across the slope of the canvas, patterned oriental by the leaves of elms. She smelt the carbolic wool that wiped the needle, and felt her buttock painted with tincture of iodine.

Dead flies hung on fly strips at the entrance to the staff sick tent, but at least, she told herself, no mosquitoes were audible or visible. Her dress was bunched in her fists and her drawers had been lowered. It was a childish pose of helpless submission. Smithy plunged the needle into the exposed buttock and Stella let out a yelp of pain as it penetrated the area of the sciatic nerve. Her heart banged in alarm and she wanted to curl up and cry, but she stood stiffly, defeated, awaiting the second needle. Now she was numb from the hip downward. When she tried to walk her left leg dragged and she was unable to sit.

Fifteen grains in a sterilised solution. Her indignation, her fury.

Nothing consoled her as she limped back to the pots of simmering rabbits. When cook saw her posture and racked face she instructed Stella to rest. She was advised to lie facedown on her stretcher, and there she was, sweating like a sailor, moaning to herself, and saturated with hot, unsatisfying tears of self-pity.

There were the dysenteries and the malarials and she was somewhere in between. She had imagined another version of war effort, not her own illness and incapacity.

Stella still hoped to visit Salonika. She felt it her duty as a writer to see what was left after the fire. Apart from when she landed at the port, and had a couple of hours to herself, she'd been only once to the city, a few weeks before it burned. It was abuzz with charm—*charmant!*—and the miscellaneous peoples and soldiers of many nations. There were markets and shops that sold Turkish delight, which staff at the field hospital relished and traded, cloth and brass trinkets from Constantinople, gloves from France, and an old English post office. Near the post office a small stall, owned by a crooked man in a green turban, sold beautiful paper with matching envelopes, embedded with petals. There was a rose garden, a cinema and any number of coffee houses, full of men smoking hookahs at the end of corkscrew tubes. An English bobby in a uniform, with MP on his sleeve, directed the traffic.

With two nurses from the hospital she'd shopped in

the morning near Eleftherias Square. They had lunch at the expensive restaurant inside the White Tower, where a Serbian captain ordered chilled wine for the Scotsky *sestres* and commanded the pianist play 'The Last Rose of Summer' in their honour. As an encore, he thumped out 'The Keel Row' to wild applause. Stella loved the cutlery, the white tablecloths, the obsequious waiters, and ordered roast chicken with meringue and raspberries to follow. Blow the expense.

In the afternoon she had visited the dentist. This was the reason she was permitted the visit.

Three old men gathered around to peer into her mouth: they'd never seen so much gold stored in a woman. One of them reached in and with his finger felt the lay of the bridgework. It took all Stella's will not to bite and scream. But her rotten tooth was extracted and she left soon enough with her bag of sugary sweets and writing paper spotted with petals.

In her notebook, under the heading 'Local Colour', she listed the colours of uniforms of the Allied regiments: this would make good copy for the papers at home. The blue of the French, the grey-green of the Italians, the white skirts of the Greek guards and the red fezzes of the French colonials. Everyone knew the khaki of the Tommies and the Serbs. She would include a description of the 'chocolate soldiers' from Africa and the turbaned Indians who nodded politely as she passed. The *Tirailleurs indochinois* and their funny pointed hats. A pair of minarets and a half-dozen cupolas, along with a view of Mount Olympus, would fill out the scene.

Had she been honest, Stella would have conceded a barrier. She felt apart from all she saw and from her workmates and companions. She'd expected credit and esteem from her role with the Scottish Women's Hospital but found her own skills negligible and her writer-self suppressed. Now, what she might contribute—a literary reckoning with the historical event of a destroyed city— had been denied her. She had been wounded by a needle, humiliated and laid low.

Stella must have slept, though prone, her cheek crushed into the straw pillow.

She woke to the call of a nightingale in dusky light. The tent still held the immense heat of the day, and she leant across her stretcher in half-dark to drink a mug of water. When she asked for Olive, Stella was told she was in the burnt zone with the surgeon Grace. Another exclusion. What might they have found there? What now remained?

The nightingale song was grating. It sounded

querulous and jittery. Stella longed for Australian birds, for the kookaburra and the curlew, for birds that rasped with rude energy and unmelodic cry. The nightingale was in full voice and threw its song towards her like a weapon. She would note this down; she was extra-poetic in her unhappiness. No nightingales in Australia.

Stella was in pain and miserable and wondering why she was here. She was thirty-eight years old and felt that her life was over.

IN THE FALLING dusk Stanley was thinking of the boy with the harelip. He wondered what saint the boy had carried in the palm of his hand. Some gentle, wise man, some holy ascetic, with a head full of angels and miracles and the presence of God. The boy might have been a mini-saint himself, marked on his face as different, as if pressed by a ghostly thumb. Finding in ruins, perhaps, what glimmered as spirit.

Boy-life, he knew, had its own intensities. He'd often rested his head on the windowsill, looked down at the field of grazing cows, to the sound of his father below, playing Bach at the piano. He was entranced by their plump, immobile bodies, the black blobs on their white sides, their low mournful groans. They were languid and complacent; they chewed with sloppy pleasure. They too listened to Bach. He had sketched them early, when he was barely old enough to know what sketching was, since they carried the secret of other beings he could not quite get an idea of. His family was lucky to have a house overlooking a field, and in the distance lay the river, the mighty Thames.

Stanley believed that their village was a site of mystical confluence. In winter they were often cut off by floods: the watery meadows bogged and became a sheet of glistening water. He remembered his family in retreat at the top of their house, and kind neighbours in rowboats who stuck loaves of bread on poles and pointed them up to the windows. When the water receded the fields and meadows were all the more lush. Wildflowers sprang everywhere and the cows once again were happy. In summer he swam with his brother Harold in the Odney weir. They saw the brown water stippling and striping their bodies. They kicked their legs and wallowed. It was Stanley who saw this as evidence of divine light. He told his brother. He raved.

Father was a music teacher and organist in the Anglican parish church. Stern and learned, he introduced his son to the writings of the poet-priest John Donne; and John Donne, Father said, was another kind of saint, who knew that death shall die, who measured in airy thinness the relations between souls, whose business was to rectify the world's corruption. He was fond of quoting *What if this present were the world's last night?* as a means of showing his son, goggle-eyed at the very thought of it, another temporal dimension.

These might have been boyish obsessions, magnified and unreal, but Stanley continued into adulthood their lovely associations. His first painting hung for exhibition was of Donne arriving in Heaven. Heaven was chunky men standing about, slightly diagonal, in long robes, thinking. There was a wide green field and not much else to speak of, but Stanley showed that pensiveness was close to godliness, that the arrangements of space between people and their angles of inclination, like the fixed and moving prongs of a drawing compass, were enough to reveal divine circles and implied connections. Donne was the hero of his intellectual life, such as it was, composed between drawn lines and sloshes of paint. At the Slade School the other students thought him unhinged, barmy with both religion and homeliness. They were full of taunt and bully and insecurity. But he was sure of his stroke, sure of his colour, sure with rare conviction of the manner and topic of his paintings. He was twenty years old when he painted John Donne. It was 1911. Even then he knew his vocation with more certainty than any priest.

In half-light Stanley touched the mules' bodies and stroked their warm flanks. Some had raw injuries where ropes from the cacolets had rubbed. He mopped at the sores with iodine and applied rough plasters. The mules were too heavily loaded—he'd complained before, but no one listened and only George appreciated his opinions. No longer officially in the medical corps, he retained his caring role and the mules were essential for moving the wounded from the Front.

They were restless, snorting, shifting their tired feet; but they trusted his touch and crooning assurances, and leant near when he called them. Whatever community they made, merging in the darkness, a link of toil and capture and the animal drag of the war, Stanley felt he respected them and was in turn understood.

He was apart from other men and always would be. He was the only man in his regiment to refuse the ration of rum. He rarely smoked. He did not curse or lament. He had never been with a woman. His drawing and portraiture were skills to be admired, but these too were a mark of his irremediable difference. At the Front what he'd seen had tested his faith; there were times he was reminded of the world's last night. And, though he believed, it became more difficult to keep the faith. He averted his gaze from the wounded, even as he tended and lifted them. He hated it when the dying wanted him to hear a curse or confession. Final words were rarely uplifting and spoke of nothing holy. Often as not, men breathed out their fear and it was secular and dark.

Stanley was permitted to administer rum if he thought they wouldn't pull through, and this was what he did, in generous amounts, to quieten them down. A gruff, drunken mumble was easier for everyone. Sometimes he stirred the rum into condensed milk and fed it with a spoon. He saw how like children the dying sucked and were subdued with the taste. At such times he thought of himself as a kind of mother.

What kept Stanley going, and what in the end he clung to, was the memory of a particular flower garden at the centre of his village, whimsically planted according to shapes and colour schemes. In his mind he recreated this garden, sometimes shifting the composition—moving the lilacs to the back, introducing marsh lilies, stalking a droopy sweet pea. He placed miniature white roses at geometric intervals and set posies of pansies along the borders before he undid his work; then he started again.

Within minutes of feeding the mules, Stanley was fully returned to his human thoughts. He held a torch to watch his step as he found his way back to the camp. Beyond the small circle of light he cast, he could hear the scrawny bushes murmur with soft fingerings of breeze. From somewhere far off a nightingale started its trill.

Keats: *Lethe-wards had sunk*. Lethe-wards; this interested him.

But the dark was swiftly increasing, and he would soon be left unpoetic in his own loneliness, as he failed easily to fall asleep.

Stanley unwound his puttees and laid the stiff smelly canvas aside. He listened for mosquitoes and covered his face as best he could. He must write to his father. He must read his Bible. The small type offered tiny insect shapes he could drift within and hide.

He wiped his hot face with a cool damp cloth.

The night was huge and the Vardar wind swept in, slapping at the side of the tents, bending the flames of kerosene lamps, rendering things shivery and vague like the flicking movements in a film.

In a vision, the boy in Salonika had followed him. And though he wanted it so, wanted a physical confirmation of faith, Stanley knew in his heart that this boy was not a saint.

He knew that this boy was outraged and powerless. Wretched, and like the war-dying, with a nightmare in his skull. And for all the rum and the prayer, no meaning, right up to the end.

THIS TIME THE drive back from Salonika felt exceptionally slow.

Darkness was falling and the weak headlights seemed more ineffectual than usual. Olive, leaning forward, drove with extra care. Something had earlier caught under the chassis, some burnt lump of a thing, which might have been wood, or metal, or the charred body of a small animal. She wanted to make sure they arrived before her vehicle seized or broke down.

Grace was no real companion, being silent and gloomy. Olive found her unreadable and felt the weight of her aloofness. And only now was she thinking again of that first night of the fire and wondering what happened to the old man who sat directly behind her, thoughtful, solemn, clutching a mirror between his knees.

Olive had spent most of her time in the unburnt sector, driving between depots and stores. She loaded all the provisions the Scottish Women's Hospital was allowed. Though some had been saved, immediate rationing was imposed after the fire, and if there was a flare-up in the fighting or a recommencement of bombardments, they'd be left short. Fuel was also a problem; she would have to source more petrol to keep her ambulance going. She would need to be practical and guard all they had. There might be food shortages too, and the loss of their mail service. What would they do if the quinine ran out?

She had driven the rubble-strewn streets, sometimes stopping to command a soldier to clear the path, or to check something under the lorry or on the side of the road. She had looked with despair at the map of the city. She recognised the street configurations, but with buildings gone Salonika was a pattern of gouged spaces, the empty frames of foundations and the half-remembered shapes of what had stood above. Often, her lorry idling in a stuttery rumble, she paused and asked herself: what had been here?

Oh, the cinema. The cinema had gone. Only weeks ago she'd seen Charlie Chaplin in an army film, *Zepped,* in which he warned comically of zeppelin attacks and how to avoid them. His doll-like eyes, dark rimmed, kept scanning upwards to the sky. At one point, smirking, he raised an umbrella above his head.

'Pity about the cinema,' she tried. She heard herself husky with emotion.

But in the cabin, beside her, Grace remained silent. She seemed dazed by her day in Salonika and inwardly distracted. Olive asked a question or two, but was met with the barest response, so gave up. Unused to discerning

British class conventions, she'd sometimes offered a comment or opinion, only to discover she had too clumsily addressed her 'betters'. The Scottish Women's Hospital claimed it was free of class but no one believed this, and figures like Grace remained hieratic and remote. No one knew anything of her background, but she was posh-speaking and a surgeon, so they all assumed that she came from money. Olive's father may have been wealthier, but it was not an Australian boast; at home money was not the shiny asset of a higher class.

When they arrived back at the field hospital the tents were lit with a welcoming gleam. Something had happened to lift everyone's spirits. Rabbits. Before they pushed open the heavy lorry doors they smelt the rabbit stew, and even Grace relaxed, anticipating a feast. They did not unpack the ambulance immediately, but sat in the staff mess, side by side, and tore at the stringy meat, bitterly amused at how unseasoned it was, and how poorly cooked. Still, it was meat, and they were tired and vehemently hungry.

'There was a man with a mirror,' Olive began.

'A mirror?'

'On the night the fire started he was in my ambulance. He had a sense of purpose, just holding on to the mirror.'

Grace barely glanced at her. 'Purpose?' Now she sounded ironical.

'It's hard to explain. In rescuing the mirror, he had proven something to himself. He looked like a man proclaiming the importance of a family treasure.'

Grace shrugged. Then she gave a throaty laugh. 'Treasure!'

Olive hated her then. Not to hear what was being said, not to realise she told the story because she was dismayed by what was being burned or blasted or raided by burly soldiers. Of all that was gone. Was going. Would never be retrieved. Grace seemed to have no regard for the dense world of sentiment, for small, fragile and personal things. Nurses said it was the work: to saw through a man's leg or stitch thread across a fleshy hole you had to lock down feeling, you had to be exacting and crafty.

Grace waved her fork, about to say more, but then apparently thought better of it and took another mouthful. Olive looked straight ahead. It didn't pay to cling on to minor slights or insults. There was work to do and this night, after the visit to *ta kammena*, they had a meal and a place to lay their great weariness.

It may have been the feed of rabbit: Olive was tunnelling backwards.

Apart from the big house in Sydney there was a family property, a cattle farm in Armidale, across the mountains. When they visited the farm, she and Violet were let loose to explore and to play without the nanny, unsupervised. She delighted in the horses and the freedom of a long country paddock with a stand of acacias and thick greyish scrub. Bolder than Violet, she was enlisted to feed the chickens, and it amused her to see their nodding heads and their bright eyes flicking sideways, to watch their podgy bodies waddling and their scary feet scuffing, to enjoy the fluff of their feathers as she hurled a brick in their direction. All startle and scamper. She did not mind seeing the farmhand, Leo, chop off their heads with an axe, since she felt no emotional attachment at all, but it was a messy business and she was given the task of scrubbing the wooden block clean. The gurgle of a dying chicken was an impersonal sound, nothing human, and without obligation, so she felt rather proud of her work with Leo. Her father told her that she was as good as any boy, and she relished his praise. Even then, she knew that she was the favourite. She would carry the floppy dead chickens to the kitchen and hand them to the cook, Mrs Maroney, who wiped her hands on her apron, took the handful of chicken feet and also praised her.

~

A rabbitoh visited the property from time to time with his cart slung with carcasses. Unlike the chickens, the dead rabbits stank to high heaven. Olive never learned his name—he was always 'the rabbitoh'—and she was a little afraid of him. He was grim-faced and secretive. He chewed tobacco that he spat in long streams, he wore a mask of dirt he didn't bother to clean, he had a gammy arm and now and then got the shakes. War injury, her father said, and it was only as an adult that she understood that he spoke of the Boer War. Injury elicited her father's respect, so the rabbitoh would be given tea and bread on the verandah, and Father yarned as if he knew him, and seemed almost deferential.

Mrs Maroney was also afraid of the rabbitoh.

'Keep your distance,' she whispered to Olive. 'Keep your distance.'

Now the wind was fast rising and low clouds were blowing across the moon. Orderlies had unpacked the ambulance before Olive finished her meal. When she stepped outside, the night had changed. Tents were buffeted and lamps guttered as if their world had been given a shake. The sky appeared to be sliding downwards and falling away to the west. No stars were visible and the moon was obscured, yet if she peered to the north, into the darkness, she saw the white line of the lake, softly aglow in the distance.

She would find it hard to sleep. Burnt Salonika was still with her. The headless chickens. The rabbitoh, that early, enigmatic fear: all were still with her. And Mrs Maroney, still whispering, 'Keep your distance.'

GRACE WAS TELLING herself: if she hadn't amputated David's legs, he would have contracted gangrene. She had given him a chance. True, he had malarial symptoms and surgery was contraindicated, but in the circumstances she had made a reasonable decision. This was a field hospital; decisions were made in a tent. The man who resembled Gerald, the man who brashly grieved, could not have known—should not have known—that another surgeon might have made another decision. This was to be human, to find oneself in wartime, tired and tediously responsible, needing to make the call. It occurred to her that the guilt she felt was because she had a witness to her decision. She'd seen so many men die; perhaps she was losing her edge.

Now she must try to sleep. The weight of the day spent in the burnt zone subdued and beset her.

Even in the tent the light was erratic and windblown; the sensation was of a night on the edge of disorder. Grace half fumbled her way to her stretcher. She saw the orderly Stella, lying on her belly, moaning in her sleep. Another for the sick tent, perhaps. A malarial or a hysteric.

Freud had written of a patient wrongly diagnosed with malaria. She had gone south for a cure and in Italy met Trappist monks who gave her a eucalyptus liqueur for her chills. The cure was for her anxiety. The planting of eucalypts, Freud went on, would clear the marshy land in which malaria breeds. Might this be so? Eucalypts to defeat malaria? Anxiety appearing malarial?

Grace had underlined a sentence in this section: that in dreams words may appear as things.

This was indeed disorder: fuddled connotations, running thoughts, a wish to psychologise physical ailment.

Most of her colleagues were sleeping soundly. Olive was turned away, quiet as the dead.

A single piece of paper was gusting across the dirt floor: Grace bent to catch it and saw it was a form from the War Office, sent to one of the nurses. Agnes Burden. This was the document sent to the relatives of infantrymen, not officers. 'Regret to inform you' was printed at the top. A kind-hearted clerk had pencilled in 'Deeply' before regret, then filled the form in a neat cursive script: a name and a rank, 'died of wounds June 28th'. Two months ago.

There was a stamp, all capitals: KILLED IN ACTION. A printed note addressed to Madam:

> By His Majesty's command I am to forward the enclosed message of sympathy from Their Gracious Majesties the King and Queen. I am at the same time to express the regret of the Army

Council at the soldier's death in his Country's service.

I am to add that any information that may be received as to the soldier's burial will be communicated to you in due course. A separate leaflet dealing more fully with this subject is enclosed. I am

Your Obedient Servant...etc.
Officer in Charge of Records.

The recipient was nowhere to be seen. Agnes Burden from Manchester was apparently Mrs Thomas Burden. Widow.

Grace smoothed flat the form and placed it on the end of Agnes's stretcher, weighting it with a tin mug from the plank of objects and keepsakes they called a sideboard. She took another mug and from the bucket filled it with sterilised water. Her thirst raged these days; she was always thirsty. Quietly, privately, she thanked the non-existent god that the message from the War Office had not been for her. She knew she was cited as next of kin to Gerald, but he was safe in hospital in Scotland, and with luck would not be returned to the Front. Six more brothers were in the war, but she had not spoken to them for years, and did not know, nor would she be informed, of their lives or their deaths. Her father had died five years ago; and when she left the church, her mother had cut her off, and never wrote or wanted any contact.

In secret, all the soldiers hoped for a Blighty, a wound clean and clear, a bullet through the calf or upper arm, that would get them sent Home. Some men contrived a Blighty on night duty, standing above the parapet, taking their chances with an enemy sniper. Any hole is better, one man told her, than having your guts blown out or your head blasted apart. They all feared disfigurement, or to lose their legs. They all feared a wound in the groin. One man she tended hissed, 'Kill me, doctor'. He was a coward, she thought, when she'd seen many worse, and direly enduring. But his groin was bloody mush, and she didn't know what to say. She was irritated and he was sulky and noisily suffering. She remembered his hands, lined with dirt and full of blisters, and wondering what labour he'd been given in the trench. He asked for a cigarette. She placed one of her own between his lips and he died—a scant puff—on his second exhalation.

She'd been told they would blur, all the dying men. But what was striking was how specific the memories were, how much her mind retained of individual gestures, or words, or the splinters of another life showing in the flesh of a new wound. Some were innocent, some were fools. Some were crushed not by their injury so much as by the shame they felt in receiving it, in being handled by girl nurses and strangers and the system that took over their bodies. With their regiments they had small protective rituals and beliefs, but once at the clearing station or hospital they were a shape on a stretcher, incongruously huge in their own pain as they were tiny in the world's estimation. The satisfaction of a medal or commendation was a long way away; at this point they were vastly lonely and alone.

Dying men humming 'It's a Long Way to Tipperary'. Smoking cigarettes with barely any breath. Hiding their playing cards of naked women. Asking for their socks. Sobbing. Frowning. The reduction of existence to these few dismal signs.

Grace glanced at the sideboard to see if the communal mirror was there. It was not. Did she look Jewish? She was still considering her hypothetical, more interesting, self, the woman with the aubergine, who did not recognise her. The woman walking self-enclosed, through a desolated city.

Grace had often searched her face when she was a girl. She hoped to see what accident or misplacement had landed her in a Plymouth Brethren family with nine brothers. She had never fitted. Could she have come from elsewhere? She sat on the edge of her stretcher, slumped over her cigarette. In sallow lamplight she rested her elbows on her knees and watched her dangling hands, as men did when smoking. Her surgeon hands, deft and clever, hung in a loose basket shape as if disabled. A thin twirl of smoke rose between her fingers. She wanted to hear music to relieve her of her tumbling thoughts, to give her other, sweeter brainwaves and less sombre reflection.

Grace slept in her clothes. She fell asleep sometime after her single cigarette, not realising when the darkness spilled and washed over her. Not the first time: she often sank like this after hours of surgery, and woke to find herself blinking in white light and ready to start again.

She lifted her head when someone raised the flap of the tent to peer in. It was a Serb, finishing night duty. It was almost dawn.

'Come,' he said in English. 'Come.' He looked apologetic and downcast. His face wore the slack, lugubrious expression of one too tired to explain.

Grace hauled herself off the stretcher, stiff and bleary. Everyone else was still asleep. She felt terribly thirsty. She paused only for a minute to down a mug of cool water.

Outside it was barely light. To the west the sky was saturated black but in the east a band of yellow was forming the rays of an early fan. It would be a cloudless, still day after such a windy night. The Serbian soldier walked ahead, expecting her to follow, so she did, with no will or reason to resist.

On the ground, face up, lay the soiled body of Agnes Burden. They had pulled her from the lake. She had weighted herself with an artillery shell. Agnes Burden, widow, lapped by water like rubbish. She would be another scandal, like pregnant Elsie Fitzgibbon. The Scottish Women's Hospital was for single women. And not for quitters.

Grace had a lump in her throat. This was the orderly who had cleaned up after the man with the head wound. The man with the twitching fingers.

'Bring her to the surgery tent,' she said. Curt now, and bossy.

She would examine the body and find an alternative story. The folds of the orderly's uniform were full of greenish lake slime; her face and fair hair were blotted with rot and nicotine-coloured mud. She'd been grief-maddened and had chosen the final darkness of the lake, giving herself the special task of sinking and leaving.

Grace followed the two soldiers who carried the body between them. One had his hands beneath the armpits, the other cradled the legs.

Her turn this time, not mine.

She had adopted the pagan superstitions of the war; thankful that it was someone else.

The soldiers, doleful and slow, leant carefully as they lifted Agnes Burden onto the table. Their actions were finicky and quietly respectful. One of the men brushed a strand of loose hair from her mouth. The other straightened the skirt, pulling it downwards to her boots. Absent-minded, he wiped his hands on his trousers. Looked down at his own boots. Appeared unfocused and upset. After so many dead men, they were shy with the body of a dead woman.

IT WAS CALM when Stella woke. The shuddering wind had retreated. She was straightaway aware of her pain, and when she rose in the tent, her leg dragged as before and she felt beastly in her disablement. She was coaxing her leg to walk, but moved gawky and angular. On the farm she'd watched calves and foals uprighting themselves after birth. They showed the same lack of fluency, the same tremulous vulnerability. She would urge the stick legs to unfold and watch the anxious search for the teat. Here it felt like an ending, not a beginning.

There was an aching spot where the nasty needle had entered. She pressed on it as a child presses proudly on bruises. It was nothing to complain about in wartime, but this was a minor disaster she could do without.

Stella shuffled to the cooking tent and was thinking again of rabbits, and her father. The smell of meat hung around. Bony remains, slender and blood-streaked, shone beneath flies in the waste buckets.

'Ye look like death warmed up.'

The cook Stewart, her attempt at humour. Zdravko was tending the fire, feeding it small twigs. He turned and nodded, then resumed his task.

Stewart handed Stella a mug of sweet tea, gestured for her to sit, then plopped down beside her. She patted Stella's thigh and couldn't wait to tell her of the scandal.

Married, now dead, Agnes Burden. How she had been slid from the lake, mucky as a Glasgow wean, all mud-caked and heavy with her secret grief. Grace had taken over, the cook said, and there would be a short service this very day, it being high summer and hot and spoiling of any flesh. Rumour was Grace had written 'malaria' on the form.

'Awthin's malaria, noo,' cook declared, pleased with her own slogan.

Stella stared ahead of her. She had not felt this ill since she had contracted tapeworm on the farm, caused, they said, by badly cooked meat.

Spoilt flesh. She too was spoilt flesh.

When she looked up Grace stood nearby, holding the kettle. She was pouring herself a mug of tea. Her face was dark, unEnglish. Stella expected acknowledgment, but the surgeon turned to her task, enclosed in the shell of her own deep thoughts, and this was another misery, not to be seen. The day stretched ahead of her. Stella was given leave of her duties and returned to her rickety bed. She would rise later to attend the service for Agnes Burden.

Her self-diagnosis was 'heart murmur'. The term must certainly describe her irregular pulse and the uneven pressure she felt in her chest. Something was not right.

More than her lame leg, more than her incipient malaria, she was a clump of disappointment, worry and fear. She was not entirely sure what it was that she feared, but when she slept again in the hot tent she dreamt of the cut-open belly of the rabbit and the shapes there, pink and snug, and her father's strange expression as he flung the pelt in her direction; then of Grace, dourly foreign, telling her she had not done her homework.

The service was short. In late afternoon, half the staff, fifteen or so, assembled at the graveyard that served the hospital. No more than a barren patch of white wooden crosses, it showed the recent addition of the amputee's mound, conspicuous with newly turned, darker earth, and another, a Serb who died on the operating table. No staff came here unless it was to farewell a nurse. Agnes Burden joined four other nurses, all dead from malaria, all with their names scratched with a nail into already flaking paint. Name and dates, nothing more. Relatives would never come.

The body had been placed in an open, shallow grave, wrapped neatly in the shroud of a new cotton sheet. An extravagance, given how short they were on sheets. She was a package now, Agnes Burden, and Stella thought of the earth that might cover her, and of how small Agnes looked, and how remote and forgettable, covered over like this, bound in a cotton cocoon.

There was no priest or minister, so Matron took charge. The women squinted in the glare and stood in lines, waiting for dutiful words to commence. For the occasion Matron improvised a quasi-religious speech. She quoted hymns dimly recalled from her own childhood and changed them into homilies and instructive lessons. Light against Darkness. Valley of the Shadow of Death. Perilous Life. Then she moved to war talk. A young woman, in service to the Allies, Cruelly Taken. The bravery of wartime nursing and the scourge of malaria. Stella heard the misdescription and knew they were joined like hostages in the conspiracy of the lie.

They ended with the Lord's Prayer.

Kingdom Come. Will be done.

It sounded like Empire. Stella noticed that, like her, neither Olive nor Grace joined in. But as the orderlies shovelled the first of the dirt, Grace stepped forward and dropped a small ikon into the grave. Stella could not see which saint was depicted but was surprised to witness what might be evidence of belief.

There were sniffles and blowing of noses. No one openly wept until Stella became discomposed. It was the fall of earth that shook her.

She let out a loud sob for a woman she barely knew and as if her voice was a breeze from the ocean, a sudden new weather, it roused others with a kind of invisible comfort. Other women began weeping. Matron was cross and stamped her foot. But the weeping women did not cease, even though they tried.

Like Stella, they wept for more than Agnes Burden.

Stella wept for herself, standing crippled and sore. She wept for envy of Elsie Fitzgibbon. Wept too, she now realised, for her own dead mother, whom she had seen covered by dirt only days after her eighth birthday, in hard-edged light just like this, on an afternoon just like this, and beside a shaggy eucalypt from which, indifferently, high birds sang.

A LOAD OF rabbits arrived, a gift from Melbourne, apparently.

Unexpected gifts always made the men excited, but this one, of meat, had them almost cheering with approval. Two Australian soldiers, who looked little more than boys, had driven into their camp, unannounced, and unloaded crates of carcasses. Stanley stared at the colours and saw his painterly response to wounds: how flesh was bright and shiny, how it was streaked with blue, how filaments of ligament or fat made a tight lacework across muscle. The likeness disturbed him. He turned away. The two young soldiers posed for photographs beside their meat lorry, enjoying their peculiar status and grinning like gargoyles.

After they left, waving wildly, a bloody smell remained.

Once they'd been sent a cargo of knitted socks intended for the men at Gallipoli.

They'd heard of the defeat, of course, and the vast numbers of wounded on Lemnos, but it was now more than a year since the close of action. They were disconcerted, ashamed even, to receive belated Australian mail. Most was generally addressed, but some was intended for named soldiers. Stanley and the others tore open their packages. Socks piled everywhere. So many socks, multi-coloured and homely. There were brief, encouraging notes: Chin up! Be brave! And advance congratulations on killing the Hun. Stanley received socks and a fierce note from a schoolgirl in Coolgardie, Western Australia, urging him to 'cut off Bosh heads with no mercy at all'. Once there was a care package—condensed milk, tobacco, a pack of playing cards, toffee. One man, as if in jest, was given a package with his name on it: Edward Smith. Gingerly, he tore the paper and found there a letter included with the socks, a letter from Lizzie Smith, a sister, sending her affectionate kisses and news of their very naughty chickens. Napoleon, the rooster, had again pecked at her knees.

Blunt men, some of them, made teary and undone by a personal message.

They tried not to think about the fellow whose socks they wore or imagine someone else wearing socks intended for them. The logic of substitution. This was an inefficient war, and crude, deathly logic had made them all interchangeable. It did not bear thinking about.

Stanley knew his own singularity. What might exist, he thought, in the Kingdom of God, was no inter-changeability at all: each man, each woman, a little world made cunningly, each an original and wholly themselves.

He'd held the socks to his cheek. He smelt the lanolin there, a deeply sexual smell. He smelt too what he took to be Australian dirt. He imagined somewhere open, with a sunflower sky.

The windy night had been eventful. Beyond the rasp of the Vardar and the slap and flap of the tents, Stanley had been woken by distant gunfire and what might have been an explosion. He'd risen for a piss and then decided to check on the mules. Restless in the throttling wind, they were less nervy than horses but unhappily tethered outside, lacking shelter. Some had pulled at their ropes and tried to break away. Some bore rope burns at their necks and withers. More than usual, their eyes looked large and sorrowful.

Half the regiment was off fighting. He stood with his animals, staring nowhere.

A soldier emerged out of the darkness, blown into a stretched shape, his hair sideways, his loosened shirt flaring up, his face distorted in thin lamplight like a figure from Goya's disasters. Stanley must prepare the mules for the wounded. There had been an encounter by the river—*encounter*, the soldier said—perhaps four wounded and one already gone.

Stanley prepared the travoys. He fixed the harnesses, and loaded the poles and stretchers to be assembled later. He pulled the mules into a line. Four was all he could manage for this initial task, and now he would need help to move them on. Anxiously, he looked around and called out, but the other men were blown in the wind, or off fighting, or refusing his call.

His mouth was open, full of wind, as he pulled the mules into the gale. They were stolid, reliable, but reluctant to move. Trees writhed and blown leaves were flung all about; moan and creak, Vardar noise, scared animal and human alike. Stanley, his arms taut, yanked the joined mules along a barely visible path.

Dark wood. *Selva oscura.* Found myself in a dark wood.

This seemed a nightmare he was in, and he was a boy again, and afraid. He might have been dissolving when a spectre, tottering pale and waving, appeared before him on the path.

Ah, George, dear George.

Together, they bent forward and tugged and shouted like demons.

It was the usual trouble. But the wounded had been lined

on the ground, waiting for them, and arms sprang out to help lift and secure them to the stretchers behind the mules. One man, Stanley judged, was already past it, but he said nothing and continued to work methodically: adjusting, tying, hollering instructions into fuzzy mule ears. He considered the load and the incline and the loose sliding soil—hazardous—but knew that they must move on.

George was kneeling by one of the wounded, saying something or other, but Stanley did not look at the faces nor move to see who had been hurt. He needed simply to work. To encourage his animals. To keep fixed on the task.

On the journey it was Stanley who was most afraid. The noise was immense: a blast and machine-gun fire somewhere. Did he imagine that? Why then at night? Ditches lay each side of the mule convoy and bullets cracked near their heads. One of the men called out with each jolting step, but nothing could be done to make the journey smoother.

He should have seen it coming. Crossing a bridge of planks slanted upwards, the lead mule, Lively, had slipped. Its quarters jammed in the bottom of a deep trench and its forelegs extended over the ground in front. The travoy tipped at a terrible angle and the wounded soldier fell from view. It was George who leapt into the ditch and pulled the man from beneath, but the animal was wedged there, jerking in its tight captivity. Others took the casualties to the dressing station; Stanley stayed for two hours, digging and hauling, frenzied by his mistake. Lively could not be saved. It was exhaustion, or shock. There were foam flecks at the muzzle and a rolling eye. The mouth gaped and stuck open. Lively heaved a slobbery sigh, bowed his head and went still.

Stanley made his return in the windy night. He watched his legs move under him, one two, one two, and felt profoundly tired. The mules were waiting. Stanley stopped to see that the wounded were properly delivered, with little cloths of gauze placed over their faces to protect them from mosquitoes then gathered his mules for the return slog to the river. They moved two more of the wounded, again passing Lively, ugly now and possibly beginning to bloat, stuck deep in the shadows of the gullet-like ditch.

Just before dawn, hostilities ceased. There was the low sound of equipment pulled away into the distance. Most of the men remained in the trenches and Stanley stayed nearby, with the mules. Star needed settling. He threw his arms around Star's neck.

Stanley couldn't sleep. He sat beside his weary animals, sheltering, and mourned for Lively.

WHEN OLIVE LOOKED about, it seemed that everything had changed.

After the howling night, and restive with figments of burnt Salonika, she was hardly surprised to hear Grace, morosely huddled over her tea, announce the death of one of their own. A night such as the last might indeed herald or contain a death. Grace glanced up, baggy-eyed and tired, and said simply, 'A suicide, overnight,' and Olive had been left wondering who, and why, and if it had been the torment of the wind, or what knowledge of the event in any case Grace might have possessed. In wartime, suicides massively decreased. Historical fact.

There was Grace, not naming a name. Offering no detail or explanation.

A chill swept through her. They were all susceptible to sudden and meaningless elimination. Olive drew back. It was then still early morning. She wished to question further, but would wait, and bide her time, and try to forget all that had recently surfaced.

By afternoon she knew: Agnes Burden. The funeral was a travesty—the easy lie of the cause of death, Stella blubbing like a child, Matron's blathering speech in which clichés knitted cosily, like socks. Then Grace, unprompted, tossed a holy picture in the grave, as if it was her role to be priestly and bless the degraded dead.

Already the talk of Agnes Burden had sorely diminished her: how could she, didn't she know, poor thing, so foolish.

The women's tent hospital, like soldiers' camps, was hazy with gossip and the fog of speculation. This occurred too after Elsie Fitzgibbon. Who had done what, and where, which sexual experience or proclivity, who had been wounded or had lost someone, or was cracking up under the strain.

On the morning of first day of fire, before they all knew what was to come, Olive had been told of a zeppelin crash. It had been brought down by British Navy anti-aircraft fire at the marshy mouth of the Vardar river. A French soldier who worked as a clerk at the depot spoke with great excitement. He had seen it himself. It was a *squelette*, he said.

At first she had not understood his meaning. *Skeleton*. The shape of it, the exoskeleton, as if of a huge, blundering insect. The German crew survived and were taken prisoners of war, the clerk went on, but one, maybe more, was now counted as missing. Pathé had been there, he added. Within hours the crashed zeppelin had been filmed and would be shown in a newsreel at the cinema.

'*Peut-être que je suis là aussi?*'

The clerk grinned, imagining himself on screen, standing self-important, arms akimbo, in front of the impressive wreck, which rose in a modern curve of struts and girders behind him. Evermore archival. He had a wiry blond moustache and his cheeks were pitted with old scars. He was thin and weedy. A man suited, Olive thought meanly, to a desk job and the promise of spectacle, rather than to the field of combat. It made sense he would speak like this, artless and jovial, of visiting the wreck as a kind of sport.

The depot office was poorly lit. It was like others she'd seen in Salonika, marked with soot from lamps, and with high square windows fitted with curtains of some pinkish oriental fabric. There were grimed bookcases, tilting, and paint hanging from the walls, like peeling skin.

Before she left, the clerk showed her bits of metal retrieved from the crash. He said they were part of the engine, 'Maybach HS'. He was proud to name it. There was some sort of piston and a piece of lever, with nothing to move. The clerk claimed he had sat in the gondola section, still partly intact. *Intact.* It sounded more important in French. And that he'd met four Canadian nurses who arrived to see the skeleton too, and had to hitch up their skirts to walk through the marsh. They were stained muddy and he gave his hand to help them up onto the metal frame. They sat in a wobbly row and he took their photograph.

The clerk placed the souvenirs on his desk to show their importance. What had been part of an airship was now this small chunk of trophy weighting a stack of papers for wartime orders and requisitions.

'Maybach HS,' he repeated, as if offering a secret code.

When Olive left, a black soldier from Senegal opened the door for her, his arm reaching as if in the beginning of an embrace. Like a servant, he bowed. In the minimal light his face was obscured, and Olive, embarrassed, thanked him excessively and hurried away.

So this too was what Olive was carrying inside. She'd not really known Agnes Burden, who arrived when Stella did, and had been with the hospital for only five or six weeks. But at the funeral, which distracted her with falsity and misconstrued sentiment, with her guilt at not grieving, with her sense of how suicide violates natural laws, she was thinking too of Salonika and the clerk who said *squelette*. She was thinking with bewilderment of the Senegalese soldier who stood in shadow by the door. And she was recalling the night in London when the zeppelin had been so close, when they had chased it in the taxi, when she too had loved the chase and would have pursued the airship to the end. Burning Salonika was not bombed London, but she had the intuition of a truth exemplified in burnt zones: of the foul enjoyment of destruction that made men rush over a parapet with a will to kill others, or drop explosives on civilians from a deadly sky.

After the funeral a few of the nurses and orderlies gathered for a cup of tea, and the talk became more subdued and generous. Agnes had been kind, they agreed, and had a sweet, helpful nature. From Manchester, they said. Twenty-four years old. She grew lovely in retrospect, muzzy and thin with the intervention of memory. Olive remembered that Agnes had worried about her boots. She had given her advice on this most ordinary of matters, but otherwise had little contact. The wife kept to herself, they all agreed.

Olive walked back to her ambulance to check the oil and water. It was shelter of a kind. She lifted the bonnet and pretended to tinker. All the stores had been removed from the vehicle, and she peered into its empty belly as if expecting to find a body left there. At the hospital depot she checked the lists of provisions and squatted outside to light a cigarette. She stayed down on her haunches, flicking her ash, casual and adrift, staring at the lines visible in her oil-stained hands.

Rabbitoh, Salonika, *squelette*. Away from the others she was more vulnerable to her raddled and racing thoughts.

The air was calm now and the elm trees were still. The lake was a peaceful slot of light in the distance. The tents all stood steady. They had room for two hundred and were almost at capacity, but more than half the soldiers were in hospital for malaria. Fear of blood infection was unlike other fears; men dutifully took their quinine but became truculent and fatalistic when the chills and fever set in. When they were told it was not a disease, but a parasite, not bacteria or a virus, but a microscopic bug, they were uneasy in their responses and grew ashamed. Some would die, ending in a coma. Most would recover.

She could hear a patient calling out, 'Sister! Sister!'

There was always someone calling out. She had promised to find a walking stick in Salonika for one of the officers but had forgotten. Now she would have to face him and invent an explanation. Most plausibly, and perhaps truthfully, that the shop he mentioned, a fine establishment with a window display of umbrellas, hats and canes—the one with the curly golden sign he had told her to look out for—had burned down. No more walking sticks. None. No more umbrellas.

'Sister! Sister!'

Olive thought of her sister, Violet, who now had a daughter, Claire. Violet's fear in the car. Her not wanting to see the zeppelin. The way she leant into the body of her husband, being led up the steps to her front door. Then Olive thought again of her own complicity. How her heart had raced. How she had stared at it, awestruck.

A meat scent was circulating. Stewart was preparing rabbit again. No doubt there were a dozen more rabbit meals to come, and they would gobble, then grow sick of them, and then vigorously complain. At some stage, they would begin to make stupid jokes about rabbits.

WHY HAD THIS suicide so affected her?

Grace remembered Agnes Burden shaving the head of the disfigured soldier, how she had bent the ears forward, how she had dabbed at his skull. How, quietly distressed, she had cleaned up after the death, moving her soggy rag in a slow circular gesture. She'd looked peaky and afraid. She'd turned away.

Did Grace even speak to her? She could not recall a single word of conversation, but felt in any case there was offence in giving up when they were all committed to saving lives, and something alarming in such grief when they had all practised suppression of feeling.

'Suppression of feeling'. It was a phrase she'd heard since childhood. God requires of us, her father had said, suppression of feeling. He had been walking in the winter garden, his hands clasped behind his back, and like a preacher he had preached. His entire conversation was of instructions, prohibitions and submission to a Higher Power. Like her, he was dark and held a rigid posture. The black whiskers that flared at his cheeks were the sign of religious ferocity. Grace waited in silence. The garden was stark and bare, the air cold and crisp, and blown leaves tangled with a skidding, soft murmur at their feet. The knot of his hands unclasped. He stopped and turned to face her. Her decision to pursue medicine did violence to him, he said. Violence.

Later, she'd joked with Gerald about killing her father, and about his habit of repeating words for emphasis.

'For emphasis,' Gerald repeated sternly, and it was a relief to both of them to assassinate their father in jest, to reclaim their dissenting minds and intentions. Father's formidable composure scared them; as much as their mother's bedridden slovenliness. At the funeral of the drowned nurse she had remembered 'suppression of feeling' and, newly acquainted with Freud, or perhaps merely yearning for explanation, grew self-reflective. Her masculine family had spent their lives in this practice, and it may have enabled Grace to work as a surgeon. Necessary for competence, perhaps, the suppression of feeling. Holding one's nerve.

Yet at the funeral she also felt disquieted. In her pocket lay the ikon from the little boy in Salonika. On impulse she threw it into the grave: an expulsion, or a dedication, she was not sure which.

The ikon flipped as it fell. The dirt falling on the wrapped body was clotted and loamy.

After the funeral, at the campsite, all were subdued. There was a rustle of hushed talk from the mess tent where a small group of nurses was sharing tea and gossip. Grace never joined such talks; she held herself apart. She must look for the Australian orderly who had wept at the graveside: the woman had the viscid pallor of a malarial and should be ordered to rest. Her behaviour had been infantile and reprehensible. She'd led others astray, she'd destroyed the dignity of the funeral.

'Stella,' the woman said, giving up her name in a whisper. 'Outlander,' she added.

Grace had not heard this expression before. Colonial, presumably. She announced what everyone already knew: that this woman was a malarial and should be confined.

'But I had the injection.' Stella's voice was imploring and weakly assertive.

'Too late, I'm afraid. Too late.' Grace heard her own, incorrigible repetition. The black mutton-chop whiskers. The violence to Himself.

Orderlies lifted the Australian woman from her stretcher and Grace followed as they led the way to the staff sick tent. Stella appeared to be lame. She was half lugged and had to be helped as she folded into herself. Grace saw that she was a make-do, stick-it-out kind of woman. Colonials had this much, she thought, native gumption and dogged persistence.

Plasmodium falciparum, Plasmodium vivax: the current wave was *vivax*. The *falciparum* strain would arrive in a month or two. She was keeping a record: ten per cent of infections would be fatal. They must secure and preserve the supplies of mosquito nets and quinine.

Grace checked Stella's heart—cardiac dysrhythmia. She would organise monitoring of her temperature and fluids. It was difficult to know at this stage the severity of the case, but Grace had seen by her gait that the woman was suffering from a misplaced injection and needed the consolation of a knock-out bromide. She left Stella to sleep.

No big operations this evening. But there were the usual prone men wanting her to engineer their magical redemption. Some arrived at uttermost dissolution, minus a limb or torn in the belly or face. Such men were prepared in their extremity, and with little feasible option, to believe a woman surgeon might save them or at least arrange a trip Home. An orderly stood rolling bandages and another was setting forth the quinine regime: six grams for each patient. Grace's task was to assess the recurring malarials, 'the chronics', for evacuation and repatriation. Hundreds each month were being sent back from the Eastern Front, their red blood cells frothing, their spleens and kidneys puffed, their hands pale and trembling like nervous schoolboys.

Chronics. 'Aren't we all?' she might have said to Gerald. It was an uncharacteristic moment of identification.

The tents were dingy at this time of the day. The light was granular and brown, the chronology gone. Soon, the lamps would be lit and her patients would falter into brightness, revealing faces turned towards her, in hope or forlorn. Wartime contained these intermediate spaces, where the injured and unlucky waited to be brought back into recognition, where their watches, if they had them, had stopped in the no-time of combat, where their dismantled lives were now all gathered in one tiny place, on a stretcher, in a tent, in stinking-hot Macedonia. They awaited letters and words that might address them by name, or restore from the boredom of their condition elements of a home or a future. That other life of frowning men. That self that walked into a pub sloshing with sour ale and bonhomie, and a man in the corner, a fixture, playing a game of chess with himself in beery half-light. Or a room, a mother's sitting room, with curtains displaying the broad faces of Dorothy Perkins roses, a quilted cushion here and there, and a teapot and lace doilies on a tray used only for guests or special occasions. There would be a pet, an old dog, snuffling half asleep by a low fire, its back leg shivering.

And what self did the Serbian or French soldiers miss? What the Senegalese? The Indochinese? She could not imagine. Grace realised then the national limits of her knowing, how this homesick anguish attached only to her compatriots.

Now too there was the stink of human excrement. Dysentery.

And now Grace was thinking again of yesterday, of burnt Salonika. And the puzzling woman with the aubergine, who continued walking away, and the grubby boy with the harelip and the air of one doomed.

She returned to check on Stella. Yes, deep sleeping. The heart in its blood-bag was still somewhat bumpy. High fever. Quivering limbs. A wan, drowned look. Not long ago, she'd seen her swimming in the lake with Olive. But she had no wish to think of the lake now, or recollect her cousin Ruth, or contemplate the defenceless body of poor Agnes Burden, washed downwards by grief and covered over by slime.

'AWTHIN'S MALARIA, NOO.'

Who said that? Cook. Stewart the cook said that.

Stella woke in the middle of the night. At first she had no idea where she was, but knew simply that a fever was raging, her head and limbs ached, and she felt the viscous flow of what might have been menstrual blood or diarrhoea. She touched below and discovered a sticky smear of blood. In the dark she licked her finger, grateful not to have shat herself.

She called out for a wad of cloth for her menses, and an orderly, Edith, arrived and obliged. She felt the woman's firm hands tilt her over and push a mass between her legs, fiddling there, arranging and smoothing, before she set her again on her back. Then a cloth on her brow: Edith patting and cooling.

'Sleep now. Go to sleep.'

An accent she couldn't place. Possibly Scouse. And the night charging in, filling her with darkness, seeming to bind her to the amorphous, swoony fret of other bodies around her, all suffering in their own, entirely singular way. In the morning she would see that in the staff tent there were four other malarials, three nurses in the thick of it and an orderly from Auckland, convalescing; but for now she imagined herself connected to the soldier population, to all the men breathing unevenly in nearby tents, some like her in a high malarial fever, some mutilated, some recovering from bullet or blast.

A shawl seemed to fall over her head and smother her. She closed her eyes and waited for the sensation to pass. In the tent lamps were turned low to save on fuel and—what was her name?—Edith was bent over a lapful of knitting. When Stella looked again, Edith had fallen asleep, her chin on her chest, her body crumpled and lopsided. The knitting needles were crossed like heraldic swords in her lap and the wool at her feet, red or black, had half rolled away. It was a bleak place she found herself in, to be staring at this woman whose hair in dim lamplight was a helmet of frizz above the oval of a missing face.

Her own missing face.

She could not have said what she dreamt of. Her mother was there somewhere, in the last stages of her illness, shrivelled and pale. And her father, leaving a room. There was the property she grew up on, the brown creek, the melaleuca, the sheep in dullard sameness, impassively gazing. There was no nightmare, only distempered, apparently casual images.

The soldiers were right: this was a dishonourable illness. When Stella woke to bright light she could hardly hold up her head. She accepted a few spoonfuls of thin gruel and immediately vomited. She was incapable of the smallest actions, but called for tea, a cup of tea, and resolved to be a demanding patient. In this abjection it was possible to loathe everyone, not only herself. When she recovered, she would leave. Return to London. After only six weeks she'd had enough of the Scottish Women's Hospital.

The suffragist Hilda Macdonald stood beside her bed.

A sewn hem. Before the rabbits, before the dreadful drowning.

Stella wanted to pull herself together. She wanted to be present, to perform, to flirt, to talk, to show off her Outlander, smart-aleck self. She struggled to make intelligent conversation and mentioned Robbie Burns for good measure. Hilda was more radical than she, a socialist-atheist, she said proudly, from a working family in Leith.

But uninterested in poetry, especially Robbie Burns. She was busy, she added, and bustled away, rattling her tray, wagging her mended skirt, heading back to the world of the haughtily well.

There was a swoop of falling, as if into a chasm. The war was gone and there was only her voracious self, with her own selfish interests and her own wish to endure. In her fever she sensed how time contracted to one body. The war was unimaginable. Borders and trenches. Will to power. Weapons. No amount of Empire journalism, or talk of beautiful Serbian men, would obscure the ravage and idiocy and dreariness of it all.

Excessive sweat made her feel she was leaking reason. But at this time, eyes shut against her own distress, Stella reasonably understood her egoism and glum ambition. The earthquake in San Francisco should have been enough to show her the puny claims of women and men. She should have read the ruins. She should have known then how solid matter might be rent and unmade. She should have managed a trip to burning Salonika.

Leaving Australia, on a high tide, there was such a sense of freedom. Country-town confinement had long tormented her, and her work as a governess had none of the romantic glamour her reading had led her to expect. It was all drudgery and disappointment, and she looked into the faces of her five charges, four boys and a snotty girl, all of them lazy and insolent and believing themselves superior, and realised she must write her way into other possibilities. She was not cut out to be anyone's servant. She produced a racy novel before her twentieth year, and was both a dissident and a popular success.

Father was uncomprehending and earnest in his disappointment. He tapped his pipe to show the disorder of plans extinguished. A bookish daughter was a scandal in farming circles. He'd expected her to marry the grazier of his choice, a strapping man with lanky limbs and beet-root skin, who lifted his hat, smiled weakly, and had no clue of her rebel thoughts.

'Your poor mama would turn in her grave.'

The odour of his tobacco. The size of his hands. She'd not expected his resignation or such a banal homily.

Mother in her grave was the least of her concerns. But she learned soon enough how those images follow and compel, how the grave itself followed, with new coffins and with old. How, indeed, parents follow.

STANLEY CARRIED THE Old Masters tucked in his kit. Gowans and Gray art books at sixpence a pop. They were modest pamphlets with monochrome plates. Resting with his socks and his drawing pad and 2B pencils were what Stanley liked to call his Holy Rhymers: Donatello, Masaccio, Leonardo, Giotto, Duccio and Fra Angelico. Botticelli, he designated an honorary member, imagining a buttock-shaped cello joining an orchestral assembly. *Botticello.*

What he saw there, colourless, were simple human gestures and triangular arrangements of faces. He saw the prettification of suffering and adoration, not to no purpose, but to oblige ordinary eyes to attend. He saw how a paintbrush might imagine a prodigious story.

His faith in religious art was entirely unmodern.

At dawn Stanley rose on shaky legs and pulled the mules back towards the camp. The paths were rocky and inhospitable, the earth still falling away in clods, and he was pleased when they made it again to the stand of tall trees, the dark wood that by daylight was a refuge and welcoming. The mules treaded slowly, bearing their travoys dismantled and slung sideways on their backs. They seemed to snort more than usual, and to look around more, as if aware of Lively gone missing. Stanley wondered in passing if animals grieve. Or if, more likely, a shape had disappeared, which made them move with uneven tread and less security. Spots of leaf-sieved light played on their rough backs. They trundled, exotically spotted, their heads lowered like mourners in procession.

He contemplated the phrase: the end of his tether. He considered his own muddled feelings, and what they might stand for. His animals were making him philosophical. And though they were not really *his*, it helped him to think in this way, and to be dumb and sincere and true in his affections.

The pencil portrait of the captain had been a success. It was shown around the camp and everyone agreed it was a fine likeness. Like all artists, Stanley knew that the distinctive are the easiest to draw, and that he was due no special praise. He also realised he'd at last be left alone, now that he bore the halo of witness to their temporary faces.

'Official halo,' Captain announced, to collective bafflement.

So Stanley raved less now, his beliefs already known. When he wanted to be left with his sketchbook or his Gowans and Grays, no one objected.

The camp was quiet as he pulled the mules to their

posts. A thread of smoke rose from the rock oven near the mess. Tea, a mug of tea. He fed the mules before he made his way to find his own feed. Since the fire in Salonika, rations were smaller. He thought of the gift of rabbit meat and was grateful.

George was sleeping off the eventful night. He must have returned by himself to the camp; they'd been separated and his friend had fled. Over tea, Stanley heard that George had been inconsolable at the death of Henry Granville, the returned one, the soldier who had said 'ruination'. That Granville should be the man flung into the ditch, whom George retrieved only to see him die before they reached medical help, troubled everyone's sense of the mystery of his return. Granville told them that he had chosen to return and Stanley considered him a lesson in renunciation. He'd given up Home, so carried the power of choice. Not the choice of enlistment, but one much harder, to return to known disaster.

Later, the captain revealed that this was false. Henry Granville had been compelled to return. He was just like them, just another fated soldier.

Stanley remembered the ceremony of the shortbread biscuits: Henry handing them around, keeping only one biscuit for himself. He'd fallen a little in love with him then and wanted to be noticed. Stanley had drawn his portrait but discovered that Henry later destroyed it. He was superstitious, he said, that it might bring bad luck.

George would not be dissuaded that Granville had chosen his return. And Stanley would not risk losing George's devotion, so in the end said nothing to contradict. When George jumped into the ditch, Stanley did not know it was to save Henry Granville, this time fallen deep beyond rescue or return. He saw a body slide but looked away. There were other matters to deal with.

Too busy with Lively, he told himself. Trying to settle the others, trying to keep his head.

It was the memory of a garden at home that kept him going, but in his art books his mind drifted to somewhere in Italy. Macedonia was the only foreign place he'd been, and militarism had brought him here and kept him captured. But he liked to imagine elsewhere. He liked to imagine what it might mean to see paintings in chapels and cathedrals, to hear rhyming names ringing like liturgy from the mouths of pretty guides. Masaccio, Donatello, Fra Angelico. *Botticello*. To see an entire fresco; in original colour. For now, he was content with the illustrations in Gowans and Gray. He could still see the elements of composition. He noted how the painted figures looked immensely still. Set firm in a story, tranquil, known.

Figures leaning, not upright, caught his attention. Gabriel's inevitable tilt towards annunciation. The Madonna's head inclined over a chubby Christ. Her prostrate form beneath the cross, tragically angled.

As a little boy he'd stuck his head in the double loop at the back of a chair. Someone had shouted, 'Get the saw!' and he thought that his head would be sawn off. He remembered the terror of entrapment, as adults chided and comforted and made sardonic jokes. He went entirely stiff. When at last he was released, he was slack and useless, unable to make his own legs run away.

Something in him, to this day, hated those chairs. But he loved the stasis in the images he saw, and the sense that a head caught in a circle might be the way to concentrate on death. This illogical link would last all his life—the chair holding his head and the access to vision. He was never sure why.

George was still asleep. Closed, snoring, he had the bundled look of a child. When he woke, Stanley would console him and be a good friend. He would show him an image of Tommaso Masaccio's *St Peter Healing the Sick with His Shadow*. St Peter was simply walking by, bestowing the afflicted with the shade of recovery. There was an old man with a staff and his arms folded at his chest, in the very moment of anticipating St Peter's mystical shadow. Stanley loved his bald head, his long, Florentine nose, his solemn, hurt eyes.

This old man reminded Stanley of his father. His father who disagreed with the war, and had not wanted his sons to join up, even in the medical service. His father who taught children piano, then played Bach on the church organ, absolutist and certain in both his skill and his faith.

THE WEEKS-OLD ENGLISH newspaper was wrinkled and smudged by many hands. Olive looked up, and closed it.

Occasionally, these days, people used the phrase 'after the war'. Sheer exhaustion made many believe it couldn't last much longer. How could anyone bear it, another front, another trench, another salient, another map. Tactics. Ordnance. Howitzers. Bayonets. The inestimable wounded. The estimable dead.

Grace had told her that 'after the war' medical science would shift from the body and address the psyche. As she certainly would. Grace was planning a new specialisation. 'The fixed bayonet, alone,' she said, 'has irrevocably damaged the mind.'

(Olive had faltered then, not understanding.)

Violet wrote that 'after the war' Olive would finally get to spend time with her new niece, Claire. Brave aunty. The war. The abstract noun of an infancy.

Might she settle in London?

Her father in Australia also wondered what she would do 'after the war'. He'd not expected her or her ambulance to last this long. An unfortunate phrase, but she knew he'd never imagined her death.

'After the war,' said the Scottish suffragists, 'women will get the vote.'

'After the war,' said Matron, 'there will be a worldwide depression.' She paused before adding, 'Economic.'

Occasionally even the newspapers, reliant on jingoist sales, suggested a peaceful future. Since the drowning of Lord Kitchener, editorials wanted a culmination.

Olive was twenty-nine when it all began. She'd known for three years that war was a bloody outrage, and though Grace had spoken to her of the mechanisms that drove men to mass murder, she still marvelled at the energy inherent in destruction.

Inveterate malice and misbegotten hate. *Desolate, desolate, will I hence and die.* She found herself verging to garbled Shakespeare, even though she knew the war was impersonal and the business of strategists, not eloquent noblemen.

It might have been *ta ḳammena*, driving through those blackened, dead streets. Or Agnes's suicide, which she judged severely, as a refusal to endure. It might have been Stella's malaria. Or the ashen residue in her clothes. Olive couldn't shake the sense of doom that this morning had descended upon her. She'd been purposeful and sure; now she felt all was waste, and futile. It was an unfamiliar feeling that she would never have spoken aloud.

~

Today, at the field hospital, there was no work for her ambulance. North, near the river, there'd been overnight conflict, but the casualties had been moved by travoy to an advanced dressing station. The men were still entrenched and hostilities were sure to resume. There was also a rumour of trouble in the west. Later, she might be called upon to collect some of the wounded. No longer excited, she was heartsick to think of it. A huge traffic in wounded bodies circulated the war zones; beyond the killing fields there were any number of transfers from stretcher to stretcher, from volunteer to volunteer, from conchie to gravedigger.

Matron ordered Olive to make yet another trip to Salonika. Word was that new emergency supplies had just arrived on the HMS *Latona*, and some were to be allocated to the Scottish Women's Hospital. Petrol, they needed more petrol. There might be a wrangle over possession, Matron said. She presented a letter, which both knew was a risible token of authority.

But with this letter, this new pretext, Olive headed back along the Monastir road, all rocks and dust but a little clearer as army traffic headed north. There were oxcarts and donkey traps and refugees walking, and all parted in slow motion to let the ambulance through.

Olive loved to drive. Now, with no passenger and no bodies to care for, driving was a vacancy, a relief, into which reverie flowed as the long road bumped beneath her. The boundary between past and present, between outside and inside, was the barest quivering screen when she drove in this way. Alone in the ambulance she visited her past with an ease impossible in company. She would see her hands grasping the wheel and discover she'd steered by a blank interval into a conversation with her father, or a time on the farm, or an event with her sister. She'd once teased Violet by waving a bloody chicken in her face and blushed to recall the upset she'd provoked. There was the rabbitoh again, with the sinister curtain of dangling carcasses. And Mrs Maroney, wringing her hands on her apron, lowly moaning.

Olive had no memory at all of her mother. Nothing to revisit. Her mother did not console from a faraway shred of baby vision or experience. She was gone forever, and only Violet retained a face, which she described lazily as pretty-as-a-picture.

There was a moment, just one, of hands drying Olive's body with a scratchy towel beneath a red umbrella. This moment, ever fading, may have been her mother. Buff rub and embrace, then a lifting upwards. A seaside dome and a rosy chamber of light.

She considered this skerrick of image once again, seeking a homely emotion to yield to, but the man who 'copped it at Covent Garden' untimely returned, repeating in the vehicular din that he could feel cold at the bottom of his brain.

At such times Olive sought her German verbs.

Olive was fifteen when she and Violet were sent by their father, in 1900, to be 'finished' in Dresden. They lived in a lace-filled hotel with high windows in the historical centre, chaperoned by a great aunt on their mother's side. They learned music, china painting, German and 'literature'. Violet paid little attention to her German lessons, but as the older by two years managed a practical vernacular that bought tram tickets and chocolate cake and expressed the clichés of delight: *Ja, es ist schön!* Olive was more scholarly and therefore received more praise, but being less pretty, was also essentially valueless. There had been instructive walks with the tutors and the Anglican service in the *Dresdner Frauenkirche*, the pews of which were punitively, even primitively, hard, but the Protestant virtue therefore assured. Olive hated their stuffy rooms but adored the solid mass of the city, knowing that it would endure forever. She looked back from the bridge over the Elbe, gawking with other foreigners at the bulbed and spiky shapes, the elegant cubes and spires. Half covered by skeining mist from the river, Dresden shone silver; it appeared airborne and eternal.

Australians were curiosities; the sisters were charming in their strangeness. But the handsome tutor who told them about 'the modern age of the metropolis' saw only Violet. Olive felt it then, how unfair to be disregarded, even though it was she who was scholarly and truly interested. She remembered that Violet had yawned outright in his face. Such an intriguing recollection: her sister, in a frilled bonnet of grey moiré silk, so confident in those days and so careless of her behaviour.

In her lorry, Olive hummed a snatch of Bach's *Badinerie*, newly amused by the flagrant yawn. She hoped still to return to Germany, but now this was a prohibited desire. The Hun, the Bosch; war had exploded affinity and made European sentiment unpatriotic. There might be Germans in Dresden longing to live in London. For them too the exclusion was brutally inevitable.

The sisters agreed that women, and men for that matter, were never 'finished'. On this topic they converged. In the shadowed room in Dresden, under the sleepy gaze of their great aunt, herself a stiff monument of musty lace, they'd grown close in a way that they would carry into adulthood. Different in temperament and aptitude, they were united in wanting to remain unfinished until the end. Olive liked to sign her letters: *with love from your sister, unfinished.*

Now dust blew across the road and Olive decelerated. She was worried that the Covent Garden man would not subside. She would have him for company in another sleepless night. If he remained until evening, she would need her German language practice. She would need to remake her location, to recover Dresden in the darkness.

AT THE ENTRANCE to the operating tent a sign read: *Gift of the Ayrshire Farmers.*

Grace had never been to Ayrshire, but imagined their citizens generous and ruddy cheeked, men and women with thick, reliable limbs, hearty dispositions and tartan accessories. Their tent looked sturdy and fit for purpose in the bright summer light.

This was her domain, the operating tent. Blast wounds were the most complex; men arrived with metal and rock particles beneath their ribs and in their lungs, and she would wait as teary nurses flushed the wounds clean with a sodium and boric acid solution. The cleaning was essential, before she removed embedded matter with surgical tweezers or forceps, before any combination of debriding or gouging prepared for the job of suturing. Anaesthetised, the patients often looked dead before she began, and as the toll of her operations mounted she wondered if this made the losses easier to bear. For the nurses, in any case, it may have helped. Some she'd seen work for hours with exceptional fortitude, then collapse in a heap over a tiny detail, something that recalled the body alive, a scribbled note, or a souvenir of touching banality. One man had a chocolate coin in his pocket, the sort wrapped in golden tinfoil and given out at Christmas time. He'd kept it eight months. Another had a woman's locket around his neck. Better to begin with the dead and resurrect.

Grace was aware of her growing inhumanity. She thought it the necessary adaptation of her third year of carnage.

One of her patients had developed sepsis in his lacerated chest. She stood at his stretcher, adjudicating, and ordered morphine sulphate and rum. His eyes watered with agony as she reached towards him. Peeling back the sticky bandages, brown underneath, she wondered if the wound had not been properly cleaned. Their fault, not hers. The man was twenty or so, bravely attempting a joke in the extremity of his fear.

'Add a black pint,' he said weakly, knowing the sign of dying, that rum in a hospital likely meant no-hoper.

His head fell back. He closed his eyes. Grace saw that he had no energy left to believe he might live. His moustache, she noticed, was rather scraggly, juvenile growth or falling out. His lips were cracked. She watched as the dressings on the wound were renewed. Scissors snipped at the bandages, so as not to disturb the patient.

Grace appointed a nurse to stay beside him and hold his hand. They might have been a couple, she gazing with fixed concern, he entering a boozy relaxation in her presence.

When she stepped outside she was surprised by the balmy light and the clarity of the air, which initially smelt—could it be possible?—of lavender. A cloudless sky. There was the polluted lake, the stand of trees, the other tents from which busy women came and went with their provisions and trays of implements. From the mess tent there was the faint smell of rabbit stew. It was a kind of calm.

She resolved to write to her brother of the trip to burnt Salonika. This way she could share it; this way she could convert the sweet shop and the song and the ravaged city to amusing news. She could sort and order the bleak images that oppressed her.

During rest time, after lunch, Grace's implacable world changed. Her mail contained a War Office telegram, and a letter from a writer unknown. Grace poured herself a mug of water and sat on the edge of her stretcher, the terrible document resting facedown in her lap. By the time she had gulped her water, her hands were shaking. Her mind all dread.

The telegram was a single page, OHMS. She saw her own

name and the field hospital address. There was no 'Dear Madam', but a blank announcement: 'Deeply regret to inform you...killed in action'...a date, but no location.

'The Army Command expresses their Sympathy.'

Such a short announcement. Grace expected mention of *Their Gracious Majesties the King and Queen*, but this note was plain, almost secretive, in revealing so little. *Army Command*. She must do with Army Command.

Grace gazed at the thin sheet of paper as if it was far away and saw how, like her distrustful hands, it shook.

This must be a mistake: Gerald was still in Scotland. But in the time logic of war, she knew this was not a mistake. This was the furled moment that had been hiding from her and now appeared on a certified form. She felt nauseated to think of her latest letter gone astray and read by an official or a nosy stranger. And she was suspended in a bitter disbelieving belief, blaming the War Office for the paucity of information, hoping hopelessly that it might yet be a note intended for someone else, dazed by the language, *The Army Command*, which seemed cruellest of all.

She was in the thrall of the document resting in her lap. She poured another mug of water. She stared into space. No tears. Not yet.

Someone entered and left. There was the scuff of a skirt. Light in a triangle opened and closed.

When at last she read the other letter, it was from a friend of Gerald's, another in his regiment. He wrote ineptly, trying without success to find the right tone. Gerald had been a fine soldier, he said, and a gallant companion. Then, more personally: he spoke of you often and we agreed if something happened we would each write to the other's sister. He was killed only two days after arriving in Belgium and resuming his commission.

Still no precise location. No village or name to imagine his body into. No north or south. Grace had wanted a whereabouts.

The friend's letter went on in a strenuous ramble: 'recently recovered', 'heroism'; this was language she abhorred. In vain she read for some detail that made Gerald her brother again.

Her mind was havoc. The friend's letter was insufferable.

Grace rose stiffly, walked back into the scented brightness and returned to the hospital tent to check on her patient. The nurse was still there, still holding the young man's hand. And he was still there, irreducible, alive. The nurse looked up and with her free hand gave a neat little wave, as if to say, yes, still waiting, but the pain seems to be gone and he is resting now, and soon he will sleep.

MOSTLY IT WAS darkness.

Before she was afflicted, Stella believed that malarial fever might bring extraordinary visions and words, that it might carry an arcane or artful aspect. But mostly it was the darkness of a torrid and discontinuous sleep. Her head and body ached so that she seemed somehow to be sleeping awake, aware of her limbs overheating and sweat pooling under her armpits and breasts as she lay, eyes closed, in the long duration of her condition. When not heated, she had chills, and her whole body shook. She noted with curiosity that her head felt double its size and resolved to ask, when she recovered, what might have caused this sensation.

Olive sat beside her and talked some nonsense about zeppelins flying or falling, then disappeared again, so that Stella might have doubted the visit. It was a mad idea, the zeppelin, and she did not want to go mad. She'd never understood the attraction, why citizens of many nations went on and on about zeppelins. A whimsical thing, a balloon. She was a train-and-boat person, herself; nothing would induce her to float in the sky. Imagine the view, someone once said, but she had no wish to imagine the view, and in her mind these phrases and images hovered and pestered; she was drifting, possibly raving, following a puff of windy thought churned by a machine that may or may not have been aerial, passing over their heads.

She watched blots of light shift and collide on the stretched cloth of the tent. She saw how day moved, sometimes fast and sometimes slow. Her mouth felt encrusted. She called out for water. She was icy cold now and could not lift her own head.

There were various nurses, including Hilda Macdonald from Leith, and her favourite now, Edith, the practical orderly, with her firm hands, frizzy hair and spongy, kind face. It was Edith who wiped her and coo-cooed maternal. It was Edith who, when inattentive, began a light hum, following a sweet melody Stella knew but couldn't quite locate. Edith tucked in the corner of the threadbare sheets, and Stella remembered that the widow who drowned had been wrapped in a sheet, that it was better and cleaner than the one that now enwrapped her, that there was a term, 'winding sheet', which she had come across somewhere, Shakespeare perhaps, since she knew a little of the Bard (she would boast), and Jesus too had a winding sheet which he left behind in the tomb; that was where it was from, biblical, everything in the end biblical, all those stuffy, samey paintings and tiresome, dull stories. Something else: her mother dying, pointing in early morning to the candle at her bedside and the ivory drapery of hardened wax and saying, meaninglessly then, that some called it a winding sheet. The candle and its winding sheet, the dripped tallow rising to extinguish the wick.

'Some call this the winding sheet.'

Stella was the oldest child and summoned to watch her mother dying and now was transfixed, as if reading an epigraph on a gravestone: *Some call this the winding sheet.*

The surgeon arrived and Edith leapt up like one about to salute. Stella felt a hand on her forehead, but Grace was silent and stony-faced, with the aloof restraint of one who knows her own importance. She seemed gaunt and haunted; even Stella, infirm, saw the change of mood and wondered why. She'd seen Grace move about the hospital like the superintendent of a giant ship or a factory, scanning with professional indifference the featureless faces looking back at her. In her fever Stella saw this too, and was impressed by her remoteness, before which everyone else dwindled. And then the winding sheet again, a pang of something she could not name, and more disordered half-sleep and more unconnected images.

Stella lay overheated in looming shadows. The day had moved on without her. Still, she was thirsty. She hoped Olive would return, but she was off somewhere with her ambulance. Edith, who had inquired at afternoon tea, said that Olive had been sent back into the zone, back to burnt Salonika. From the tangled mess of her sheets, which Edith was again untangling, lifting her feet, smoothing the thin cover, Stella recalled Olive saying 'catastrophic'. The drama of the fire had enticed her and now, she thought poetically, she was all aflame.

Stella was defending herself. She was still aware of her lame leg and the pain in her buttock, and worried that she might never recover. What must it mean to be permanently at a loss? She was determined to write to her father, to return to Australia and to reconcile with her siblings.

At the funeral for Agnes Burden, she had wept in public when she looked into the grave. Baffling, the strength of her reaction, and the embarrassment that ensued. She was not even a mourner, just one shocked and alarmed: defending herself.

She wanted to ask Edith directly: 'So, will I die?'

Edith was rubbing and pulling at her feet. Stella motioned for her to stop and obediently she stopped, giving her feet a small final pat, as to a dog. Edith turned back to her bowl and tray and resumed her hum.

The melody named itself: *You made me love you, I didn't wanna do it.* The rewinded voice.

Stella had heard it when she made the day trip to Salonika. Another time, weeks before the fire. A French-owned café, somewhere near the port, had set up a gravelly gramophone on a table to play the most popular tunes. Patrons took turns at the choice and access to the crank handle. They sat in a semicircle, looking with reverence into the deep hibiscus of the horn. Excellent almond cake and music: Stella hoped to return.

It was a song of complaint, she thought, and not beautiful at all. But in the way of her darting, fidgety mind, in the way of her fever, which was as much absorption as it was distraction, she played the lyrics in her head, sad and sensual, a woman to a lover, obsessively yearning, undeterred, and with no real regret.

With her fingernails Stella had chipped at her mother's candles after the funeral. She tapped at the cold wax and watched it fall like thickened snow. She put some of the wax in her mouth to taste it, to eat her dead mother.

Snuffed light now and after brain-burst she felt herself falling: new-bereaved and lonely.

Edith placed her wrung cloths in her white enamel bowl. Still humming the same tune, she ambled away.

GEORGE HAD BEEN enfeebled by the night and woke unrefreshed. Stanley saw the toll of it, how failing to save Henry Granville from the ditch had been the one thing that had broken him. He'd said something, Stanley guessed, kneeling beside him, that promised Henry Granville another return; so that it was the broken promise as well as the awful mistake that undid him. Not an enemy bullet so much as a clumsy mockery of his body, to be flung like that, and beneath a mule.

George's huge hands wrapped around his tin mug of tea, and Stanley felt small and useless beside him.

'And Lively,' he began, but then knew this would add insult, so wisely went quiet.

'Yes, poor bugger.' George had room enough for Stanley's loss.

George swigged the last of his tea and drew a crushed cigarette from his pocket. Straightened it in his palm with a rolling gesture. Lit it, inhaled, sighed the sigh of a whale.

They would be careful with each other all morning. They went about their tasks, loading ordnance, carting the provisions, stacking the crates of still melting rabbits, some already, Stanley saw with disgust, turning green at the edges.

At the field near the camp, the company of mules stood idle. They had forgotten the night. Star chomped at his sawdust and showed no sign of missing anything. His gaze was empty. This was peace, Stanley thought, animal emptiness, lack of grieving. He gave each mule a slap on the rump to test its solidity, and none showed any response beyond a casual flicker.

Now was not the time to show George *St Peter Healing the Sick with His Shadow*. This had been his reference alone, to seek the comforting allegory, to revert in crisis to a picture that showed his father's believing face. He understood how he bolstered himself by finding faces in pictures and pictures in faces; how his art books were the reassurance of an order to chaos, how this order was an appeal to certainties that he wouldn't or couldn't examine. His father's certainties. There was humility in this understanding: before, he would have raved and tactlessly insisted; now he let George be, let him have his elegiac silence.

Stanley was not a spontaneous man, but when the rabbit lorry stopped on its way back from deliveries all over the region, he banged with his fist on the metal door and asked for a lift to Salonika. More than untypical, this was Stanley showing his new intention, which was to flee.

Now he was absent without leave. And sorry for himself.

He was wedged between the two Australian lads, who were jovial, smelly and unconstrained. Perhaps they could hardly believe their luck: to be given a lorry and freedom, along with the unearned munificence of their bounty. The taller, ginger, drove like a madman, resentful of other traffic and the poor quality of the road. He sang and spouted obscenities. Stanley couldn't bear it. The smaller was dark, subservient and smirky. They were performing for him, showing a weedy Englishman how masculinity worked. They began singing 'Mademoiselle from Armentières', *parlay-voo*. Verse upon verse. He'd heard it so often that his mind automatically played along, *Inky pinky parlay-voo*; he hated how such songs carried the crudest of feeling, set it rolling in the head like a machine, with no thought process or control. Like war, like the ruthless compulsions of obedience.

It might have been twenty miles on when he asked to be let out. He needed peace and quiet. It had been a stupid decision to join the lorry and now he would wait by the roadside until an army vehicle travelling in the opposite direction met him, and he could return to the camp. The Australian soldiers doubtless confirmed their superiority: this Englishman had not the foggiest notion, was a bumbling fool, with no conversation, and lost. He was like one returned from the Front, one of those men who'd lost their wits in an explosion, so that they were jangled inside and grappled with simple tasks and decisions.

Thoughtfully, they left him by a gully of scrubland beyond which grew a stand of olive trees, so that he could rest in the shade. They waved as they drove off, an arm flaring from each cabin window, as if the lorry in its speed had grown human wings. Dust flew up behind them and Stanley saw how rapidly they veered away.

How much time had passed? He sat by the side of the rocky road and might have begun weeping, but for the locals who passed by now and then and stared with frank suspicion. They had wasted, hungry faces and their curiosity didn't last long. There were oxcarts and filthy sheep and old men carrying French rifles. One man rode a donkey while a robed woman walked beside him. One woman, Stanley noted. A road with only one woman. This was the road of Alexander and Xerxes, but the names held no charm as he waited now, disconsolate, for deliverance and water.

An hour passed, then two. His nose was burning in the sun and Stanley wanted a sleep in the shade. He slid on the dry clay and groped his way to the gully and the trees, wishing to rest. This was not his place. No classical name rescued him or made sense of his body, half sliding without foothold, making him more fool than ever. When he found a smooth spot his knees simply buckled beneath him. Obscured, he sank and, making a pillow of his rucksack, he slept.

At first, he couldn't remember where he was; then dazed saw the olive trees, gnarled and ancient, and the dusty road in the distance, now empty of travellers. He stretched and yawned and felt terribly alone. He put on his spectacles. And then, at the edge of his vision, he saw a dead German soldier. It came to him as a horror that, thinking himself in open air, he had slept only steps from a dead man. The uniform was unmistakable and the body was curled in death pain. Blood had congealed blackly beneath a wound somewhere in his middle. Such a puzzle: why here, why only one man? Stanley lifted and slowly edged his way towards the corpse, hoping, though the thought appalled him, to find a water flask there. He would drink a dead man's water. And he could not avoid it this time, seeing the man's closed-up face.

Stanley bent to the body and gave it a little prod; and God, oh God, the eyes in the face narrowly opened. Stanley fell back, but still the undead man watched, his gaze the spear of a plea or an accusation.

He could have finished him off but did not. He could

have backed away. Instead, with a measure of inexplicable guilt, he fumbled in his mind for something kindly to say. In confusion he blurted the words of an old hymn his father had sung:

> *Als Jesus Christus in der Nacht,*
> *Darin er ward verraten,*
> *Auf unser Heil ganz war bedacht*
> *Dasselb uns zu erstatten.*

The German man looked astonished. He blinked like a newborn.

'Bach's hymn,' Stanley said, by way of apology and explanation.

He had no idea what the words meant, but the verse and rhyme had stayed with him, and the sound of his father's choir, high-circling over his children's obedient, lowered heads.

'*Bachs Hymne*,' the man repeated.

It was soon clear there was no more German language, just a patchy repertoire of childhood snatches. Apparently, the German man knew no English.

The men stared at each other. Stanley removed his glasses, wiped them, then placed them again on his nose. Still there. Both were oddly, timelessly, exposed.

This exchange in thin shade, almost languid in tone, was enough to bind their two fates together.

IN SALONIKA, AT the depot by the wharf, Olive secured sacks of flour and a second supply of quinine. She waved the letter and said 'general', 'command', 'urgent', and her fraud did the trick. Mayhem favoured the bold. The port was still functioning, though the town was two-thirds gone. The arsenal was rebuilding, as if more firepower was needed. A cache of grenades had gone up, they said, and needed immediate replacement. This was war; 'never enough' might have been the slogan of generals.

Ships came and went, supplies were unloaded, and it was rumoured additional troops of the Allied Army of the Orient would soon arrive. There would be an Eastern Front push. The White Tower remained a military centre, and treasures and antiquities of the city were held there, secure in case of air raids. In Ottoman times it had been a fort, then a prison called the Red Tower. Now parts of the chemise, the low wall, had disappeared, but the White Tower remained obdurately complete.

Olive was driving in her safe, foreign aura on the outskirts of the city when she recalled her principal mission; she would be stuck if her petrol ran out. A woman alone, and with valuable supplies. She had yet to find petrol. Beyond, Olive saw the undestroyed Tower and its high crenelations. She knew a little of the history and wondered again if it was true, that the Red Tower had been an atrocity, coloured with the blood of slain janissaries. Whitewashed now, the Tower still disturbed her.

Again, she saw that the old town of the Jewish Quarter was razed. Someone at the depot said that sixteen synagogues had been lost. More wandering for these people, more disastrous expulsion. Olive followed the shining curve of the tramlines towards what had once been a centre, and only now understood that it was the woe of others that claimed importance. The incinerated city was an entire world gone. On her visit with Grace, she'd searched for personal coordinates, the cinema, the shops, the Palais de Variété restaurant. Now, staring into the terrible distance, she saw another scale of loss, and was aghast and ashamed.

A ruined synagogue slid into view, as if to answer her feelings. Through the smudged windscreen she saw that it was bare outlines that moved her, blackened pillars and an archway stretched between them. In front of the archway stood a marble platform, which she took to be an altar. And a man sitting alongside the wreckage, unable to lift even his gaze. She looked ahead at the tramline, as if it would lead her supernaturally away, as if there was a track going backwards, back to before.

Most of the streets were still strewn with scorched debris and remained unpassable. On the main thoroughfares, teams of Indian and Senegalese soldiers were clearing rubble with shovels and wheelbarrows. They loaded carts and lorries, their clean-up role mandated by prejudice and military caste. Along corridors of waste Olive reproached herself for her lack of imagination. She saw shapes that were indecipherable and others retaining a kind of function; stone walls remained; civilian street plans were still discernible. This was not France, with deep trenches and hoops of barbed wire, trees blasted to sticks and fields to swamp; this was unmilitary fire; this was evidence that nowhere lies beyond tragedy.

When she drove now it was with a kind of sorrowful amazement. A delay had slowed her reckoning. She saw nothing everlasting.

Olive had intended to revisit the French clerk to get directions to the zeppelin. But in this new frame of mind her plan seemed a folly and a disgrace. No one would know if she took a detour, but her interest had passed. A picnic excursion, the attraction of a curiosity: these were outings for future times.

Her dark mood persisted. *Desolate, desolate.*

The clerk saying *squelette* with a thrill that might have meant a human body.

The man sunk in weary loss beside marble pillars and an altar.

Olive was overcome by the urge to flee. She headed to the petrol depot on the north-east side of the city, assessing hazard and damage along the way.

She became impatient to return. Loaded now: quinine and petrol, good as gold.

On the return journey Olive leant over her steering wheel like one peering over a brink. Her mind was dull; she calculated the miles. The road was familiar and she drove with inattention, so that she barely saw him at first, a figure running out before her, waving his arms in oneiric slow motion, commanding her to halt. It was a Tommy, apparently lost, a short man with glasses, gesticulating, grimacing, madly sure of his purpose. She braked and almost at once he had leapt onto the running board, his sunburnt face at the open window.

'Please, please.'

She could see anxiety and fanatical will but was unsure what his 'please' was asking. Cautiously, she slowed the ambulance and looked around. When they stood together the man extended his hand.

'Royal Berkshires. Stanley.'

'Scottish Women's Hospital. Olive.'

This formality in late afternoon, on the Monastir road, was the restoration of their official roles. Olive was afraid to leave her ambulance and its supplies; there had been many pilferings and outright thefts, and this was an unusually precarious time. But the man indicated she should follow—'Wounded,' he said—and she hesitated only a little before pulling a stretcher from her lorry. She crossed the road behind him, then followed down an embankment and into a dry clay gully.

She'd never seen a German soldier in this part of the territory; he was unaccountable. There were no other people to be seen; there was no human sound. In London she'd glimpsed a banner in Agar Street outside Charing Cross Hospital: 'Quiet for the Wounded'. This was quiet for the wounded, the hush of an inadmissible secret.

His condition could not be estimated, but when Stanley took the underarms and she the legs, his eyes popped open and he looked directly at her face.

'*Ruhen Sie sich aus.* Rest.'

She might have been a phantom to him, a German phantom. His eyes closed again.

~

It was hard work lifting the wounded man over the embankment. In the end they pulled the stretcher and hauled from above. Olive's mind was in turmoil. A prisoner of war. Should he be taken to the field hospital or somewhere else? He was unlikely to escape. Should they keep him a secret? Together Olive and Stanley restacked the supplies and slid the wounded man between them, his head too near petrol cans, medicines and sacks of cornflour. The sacks were the safest, Olive judged, and she wedged them as one would sandbags.

They gave him water, lifting his head gently, letting it flow in small sips.

The man called Stanley had little to say. Olive had no idea why he was on the loneliest stretch of the Monastir road with a wounded German soldier. They rode together mostly in silence. Stanley agreed to come to the Scottish Women's Hospital first, for the sake of the man, semi-conscious, possibly dying, behind them. Later she would learn about the mules and the drawings, but for now this English soldier was reluctant to answer her questions, caught in his own worried and dislocated world.

THE ARMY COMMAND expresses their sympathy: she could not get it out of her head.

Grace needed to tell someone of the death of her brother, if only to contest the annihilating impersonality of the letter. Olive, she would tell Olive. But Olive was in the burnt zone, they said, on a mission to find more supplies. The others knew she would find them: she was as formidable in her own way as Grace in her surgery.

It was evening when the ambulance lorry rattled into the cleared ground of the field hospital. Even as Olive stepped from the cabin, Grace could see there was another figure, a man sliding down and seeming to hide behind the windscreen. Olive rushed to her and whispered, and Grace peered into the back of the ambulance. It was the uniform she saw first, not the man. There was a startled moment, in her grief, in which she wanted the enemy punished. A surge of contempt.

Olive said, 'Hurry, hurry,' as if the man was one of theirs.

And then the other soldier was there, pulling at the stretcher to move it, so that she found herself acting decisively, wanting to guard them all. Grace directed the stretcher into the staff sick tent and followed, wondering if she should enlist the discretion of an orderly. The woman called Edith was already there. Edith's hand flew to her mouth when she saw the German uniform, but Grace indicated 'shoosh' with an upraised finger. It was the dumbshow of a group entirely unsettled. They all knew this stranger would not remain a secret for long but recognised spontaneously a collective task. It was the Tommy encouraging them: some connection made him protective.

Grace asked without thinking, 'What is the protocol here?'

They all looked at her as if she had spoken Chinese.

The staff patients, all five of them, were wide-eyed with mistrust. Olive calmed Stella and hoped that she and the others would keep their secret. There was a sense already of systems collapsing and precincts made bogus. The Tommy was called Stanley, Olive said; he nodded at Grace for approval, but mentally she sneered and withheld. To her he was a rude intrusion, a smuggler, a man in the wrong place.

She saw that urgency emboldened the Tommy and made him active. There he was, stripping the body, without being asked. As if he were in charge, he unbuttoned the jacket and peeled cloth from the wound. He pulled off the boots and removed the trousers as Edith drew up the sheet. They were working together, Stanley and Edith, in wordless concord. Grace watched as Edith began the cleansing of the wound, which was neither bullet nor blast, but compression and torn flesh.

Olive looked pale, as if still she disbelieved.

So what task was this? In the surgery, Grace sewed and bound the wound of a man her brother would have been obliged to kill. She peered into the body and it was a body like any other, a neat arrangement, beautifully packed, but for two crushed ribs on the left side that had broken through the skin, emerging bloody and shiny like claws. The spleen was enlarged and bruised and may have been damaged. The pulse was racing. It took all her concentration to set the ribs, mend the gap, dab with gauze, suture, bandage in a tight circle around the whole torso.

She saw his face, which was plain. He was neither handsome nor ugly, just a young man, someone else's brother.

And now she felt ragged. After surgery there was always a sudden release from tension, but this had been a rash and distracted procedure. Edith and Stanley moved the German patient onto a stretcher beside Stella, who was now back in the grip of high fever and didn't notice or couldn't have cared less.

Grace and Olive sat each side of the German patient. He lay very still, breathing through his mouth. He was disguised by a nightshirt, and Olive said that, if he stayed silent, if they all stayed silent, he might remain in their care until he mended or died. A conspiracy of sorts, a conspiracy to save.

He had the telltale frown, Grace noticed. Injury had shown him his own mortality.

She reached into her pocket for a cigarette, found two, and passed one over the patient to Olive. Then the matches, then each slumped with the effort of the day, as they inhaled and sat for a while in restful blankness. The cigarettes were French and had an acrid afterburn and the tiny spark of a crackle. Grace was wafting inside, towards her darkest thoughts. She was becoming smoke.

She might have waited, but instead simply made an announcement. 'I heard today that my brother Gerald has been killed in action.'

Olive glanced up, taken aback, unprepared.

'Don't say anything,' Grace went on. 'There was an official letter. *The Army Command expresses their sympathy.*'

'I'm sorry.'

The look on Olive's face, wrung of feeling, stark,

explicitly shocked, might have been the mirror of her own. It was unbearable to see it. Grace had relied upon Olive to be staunch and impassive, to absorb her news in a way that enabled her to be firm. But the lone trip to Salonika, or the German soldier, or the time with the Tommy, had changed something in her. With no consoling staunchness, Grace heaved with a slight shudder, then wept. It was not huge weeping, like the man who loved David, or Stella at the funeral making a spectacle of herself, but a hazy sweet release from the pressure of saying nothing, a sound like the sway of murmurous trees at night, something breathy and active, something that rose, then fell, then gently dispersed.

Edith returned from disposing of the German uniform in the stove fire. She pretended not to notice the surgeon crying. 'Who will tell Matron?' she asked.

'It can wait until morning,' said Olive. 'I'll handle it.'

Stanley had been sitting on the duckboards of the dirt floor, dopey, half asleep. He perked up to ask to be driven to his camp.

'In a few hours,' said Olive.

He did not insist. He looked resigned and sank back, seeming to make himself smaller.

Grace saw that Olive was practical and cautious in

the face of an enemy. She was allowing time to open and settle after the gripped panic of the stranger's arrival and the stress of the operation.

Surgery was necessary and she was competent, Grace told herself. She'd always refused to dwell on the vast numbers on both sides that made the battlefield unthinkable. Her brother's death unthinkable. It was how she managed to continue.

Tonight, of all nights, she was confused by the arrival of this man in the wrong uniform.

There was more that was new to her: someone else in control and the simplicity of weeping. The sheer relief.

With a lowered head, she examined her wrists and her extinguished cigarette. She wondered again about the etymology of 'lull'. She looked up at Olive and saw that she too was inside her own thoughts, eyes closed for a brief nap, perhaps already drifting away.

WHEN SHE WOKE, Edith was still there, seated on a chair, knitting. It was as if she'd never moved. Stella watched the rhythm of her quick hands and heard the minute click-clack of her efforts. The wool was jittery moving upwards towards the needles, then consumed, made wavy-linear, patterned and incorporated. A marvel to someone who had never learned to knit. Socks: Edith the immovable was knitting a sock. In the hypnotism of the moment Stella forgot her own unhappiness.

Last night's arrival was not a fevered vision; there he was, the wounded German soldier. To her right he lay, eyes closed and either dead or drugged. She had only a vague recollection. Olive had been running the show, and a Tommy soldier was hanging about. Grace was curiously passive and unsure. She'd watched as the Tommy unbuttoned then cut away the German uniform, and Edith dripped liquid, as in anointment, before her careful wiping of the body. Together in silence they had prepared the wounded man for surgery. Stella recalled nothing after that; she must have slept.

She was aware of her own stink, menstrual and sweaty and with perhaps a trace of shit. She may have vomited in the night; she didn't remember. It was this loss of control she hated most. To be tucked here, weak as a kitten, watched over, washed, consigned to the ailing mass who might or might not make it. She knew the numbers and had seen the malarial dead, but also knew, by instinct, in the ruby innards of her body, that she would not die this time.

'Not his time,' she'd heard a nurse say, in a tone of intimate admiration.

Then it returned to her, her mother, and all that she'd remembered in her fever. In someone else's story or on the stage she might have appreciated the melodrama, but this was her own private and difficult knowledge. She knew too well of her attraction to sensational stories and how they might be used or sold. She would wait for the feelings to exhaust themselves, to fall away as she regained her strength. Only then might she know what she had truly revisited.

Unnerved by her mother, who had turned in her grave, winding her.

Olive appeared at the entrance to the tent, letting in a flash of morning light.

'Just checking!' Olive attempted cheeriness but was barely upright. Her face was like marble, all strain and enervation.

She said she'd not yet slept. She'd left before dawn to return the Tommy, Stanley. That way he might avoid being discovered absent without leave. It was an hour away, the British camp, and he had mostly slept as she drove, forsaking her to anxious wakefulness and the turbulence of her thoughts. The darkness had been bleak and dangerous, she said.

Stella offered no response. Why was Olive telling her this?

'I'm cold,' she interrupted, and Edith leapt up.

Together, Olive and Edith wrapped a blanket around her, pulling it tight at the sides. It was reassuring to be a contained bundle when the events of the night were flailing shapeless.

And then Olive left. She needed an hour or two, she said. To sleep. To try, anyway.

Eager to be away, Stella thought ungratefully.

She knew only that she wanted the German soldier gone. It was a violation to have him here, dead or resting. She suspected that Grace had visited in the night to check on him, so he was likely still alive, protected by their busy and intensive collusion. She gazed gloomily in his direction and wondered if Edith was in on it. She was impressed despite herself by the organisation around her, by how medicines and cups of tea appeared, how none complained as they dealt with her bodily waste, how the quinine was measured, the temperature taken, by the whole apparatus of medical care. But she didn't want this care extended to the enemy, or to have to look at him beside her, so very close. She didn't want to share the space of the tent, her still tentative world.

The others were sleeping. It was early. When they woke, yes, there would be a reckoning.

Edith had left now and it was just the patients, alone. Stella's head was banging and she must ask for a bromide. But she had a thought or two. Civilisation was in decay. To do battle against evil one needed to maintain borders and boundaries; one needed to know and distinguish the enemy. She would write an article on this topic and try for the English papers. She would cite her experience in Macedonia as an object lesson in the dangers of relaxation. Belief in enmity, she would argue, made the Empire strong.

But then the sweating began again, and the pitch into queasy fever. It was like a cave, and she slid into it, falling through curved darkness. Dreamlike there were flourishes—her mother's face, her father's, a cloth squeezed over the dented white enamel bowl, the glint of water falling and the feel of it on the surface of her skin, outward, damp with a breeze, and slowly cooling. And fury. A kind of fury.

IN THE DARKNESS, with a torch, he had seen their eyeshine.

His mules were tethered in a clump, all looking towards him, their eyes gold-teal with an iridescent reflection. *Tapetum lucidum*, it was called. His father had named it when Stanley was a child and he had never forgotten. Given to what he called the 'true names' of things, his father often offered the Latin tag. Stanley disappointed him by showing no interest in or aptitude for Latin, but made up for it by loving Donne, and having a musical ear. Humans, said his father, do not have *tapetum lucidum*, a reflector behind the retina. Lesser eyes, he said gravely.

As Stanley approached the mules, Star scraped at the earth in irritation, setting off the others. They moved as one body, sideways, in an animal waver. They had not been fed. Stanley prepared their feed, adding more oats than usual, and in tender apology rubbed at the scar on his favourite's throat. He wished he could speak Spanish to the voiceless mule. He would offer an endearment that Star might have heard when young. The mule nudged, trustful now, and with a belly full was forgiving. Stanley checked the travoys, filled the water trough, patted each of his mules with a few hearty slaps. By these simple actions, he felt himself revive. The night had been a test of endurance and he'd felt at every turn that he might fail.

Many were still at the trenches and Stanley was pleased to return to camp when it was relatively quiet. He was in the tent with the remaining men of his regiment before they woke. Asked where he'd got to, he said he spent the night with the mules. No one inquired further. But George, who had seen him climb into the cabin of the rabbit lorry, would be keen for the true story.

Stanley planned to thwart him. Not much to say. He'd gone for a ride, then changed his mind and caught another ride back.

He took off his shoes before the others woke. It was such a relief to free his feet, to move his toes, to feel the air. His socks were those sent by the little girl who wanted him to cut off the heads of the 'Bosh'. He waved them around to release their clammy stink, then bathed his feet, carefully cleaning and drying between his toes.

He would like to paint Christ and his disciples, featuring their feet. Twenty-six feet would be at the very centre of the painting.

They were wanted back at the trenches.

The lull had broken, someone said; it was more serious now.

Stanley moved with the air of a man having forgotten something, but he was fully remembering. He felt hot all over and had a sense of malarial foreboding. And, though it was barely credible in daylight, his secret weighed inside him. He had stayed with the German soldier until he saw the truck with the unlikely and fortuitous blaze of a red cross, then leapt into its path and demanded help. That it was the Scottish Women's Hospital made him feel safe: women had less capacity to judge, he thought. He'd not expected an Australian—Olive—nor her conviction and skill. Her voice was harsh and she showed him no deference. But she took charge in the end and had driven through darkness to return him. He pretended not to notice her downy forearms as she pulled at the steering wheel, or the shape of her small breasts beneath her shirt. He found himself surly with unexpected desire. Apart from church, which didn't count, he had never before sat so close, for so long, to a woman. She knew German and was strong. She lifted stretchers as well as any man. She drove robustly and with decisive, bodily confidence. When her hand reached for the gearstick, or to push at the ebony choke, he almost seized it.

Stanley had been conscious of deep embarrassment without really knowing its cause. He recalled the playing cards of naked women that fellow soldiers had shown him. Engrossed, aroused, he'd immediately turned away even though he wanted to see more. He thought then how accurate the term 'heart-throb' was, since his heart mightily throbbed at the sight of the women, offering themselves in stagey poses, reclining or prancing with feathers and veils, spreading to reveal an enigmatic dark spot between their doughy thighs. He'd been abashed to recall them in the thundering lorry, sitting beside this woman who paid him no heed.

'They will make us culprits,' Olive had said, and for a moment he thought she meant sexual.

The trek back to the Front, pulling the mules, was arduously under way. The morning was fiercely bright. Stanley dragged his worn-out will behind him, his mind neutralised by sunlight and heat. He wanted to sleep, then to look at his Holy Rhymers. He wanted to think about Olive. He wanted to think about Lively and Henry Granville and the German soldier whose clothes he had removed. It was a function of labour, he decided, to subdue what might trouble and expand a more mysterious self; it was a function of war to make it all meaningless, these compelling attachments, these smitten loves, these challenges to regulation and uniform knowing. Knowing in a uniform.

There was harsh noise ahead. The mules plodded on. Stanley was always struck by their hunched tenacity and relentless obedience. No eyeshine now, but clear-sighted day. He would load them and they would move together with the wounded.

OLIVE WOKE TO full sunlight with the words 'Invalid Port' in her head.

Where had that come from?

And then the whole night returned, the rush to deliver the wounded German, Grace's meticulous surgery, her disclosure of the death of her brother. They'd smoked together, taking their time, and it had been a genuine closeness. She'd returned Stanley to his camp, parking just beyond so he could sneak in before dawn. Stanley was worried he might be mistaken for the enemy and downed by a sniper. It had happened before, he said, someone creeping back, furtively prowling, and then fatally mistaken.

Olive wondered if her ambulance had been unloaded. The quinine, the cornflour. Must check. Must work. Work was a solution to all that snagged at her. The barbed wire around Salonika, still standing, protecting absence and ashes, might have been her emblem.

She stood in silence for a minute looking out towards the lake. They needed rain. It was such an Australian thought, to squint into sunlit distance and wish to gauge the degree of drought. The wind was low but hot, and the lake was spoiled now. She gazed at its mirrory stripe. She could not imagine swimming there again.

Edith was beside her. 'Matron,' she said.

Olive knew she had been summoned. She would check the ambulance later.

'Quick,' Edith added, as if there was an urgency she'd not noticed.

In the tent she saw that faces were solemnly assembled and turned towards her, waiting. By their mute attention they indicated that Olive alone would restore order with the correct explanations.

Stella was awake, unhappy, staring reprovingly. The German man was also awake. It surprised Olive to see him turn his head when she approached; they looked at each other with frank, even amiable, interest. His face was drawn, alert. Post-operative adrenalin.

She saw that Grace was present, and Matron, all suspicion and disdain.

'You will interrogate the prisoner,' Matron said, 'before I inform regional command.'

Grace seemed to flinch with disquiet. Olive had not thought the German a prisoner, nor herself an agent of the army. Not only the language, but the assumptions were foreign to her.

'And Dr Grace will witness. And confirm. In writing.'

So Grace had said something. Outside, an object thudded and all were temporarily diverted.

'My work is not to interrogate,' Olive said.

Matron blinked her hazel eyes. She saw her error. 'A poor choice of words. You will ask the German man questions. We need to know if there are more of them. If our boys are in danger.'

It was a tenuous interval, with Matron anxious about insubordination, but asserting her leadership with bombast and the principle of power. 'If our boys are in danger.'

'So, I am the Grand Inquisitor,' Olive began.

The German smiled.

'Don't smile. They will get the wrong idea.'

There was a discretion they must practise, with so many observers. And Grace, knowing German.

Olive introduced herself. 'Yes, like the tree.'

She apologised for her German grammar, but the man—Jakob—said that his English language skills were a joke. *Ein Witz.*

Witz. She'd always liked that word.

They spoke obliquely for a short while, each circumlocutory, each withholding and speculating. Yes, in Dresden, as a fifteen-year-old girl. He'd visited Dresden once, and what a sight, the eternal city. He was from Trier. It was Karl Marx's birthplace, he added, with unmistakable pride. He was not long out of the *Gymnasium*, where his favourite subject had been Ancient History. He wanted to be a scholar of the ancients. The old ones. Parents.

Such familial expression.

Olive was concerned by the ramble. There was no discipline here. This was a young man eager for a chat and with no sense of how vulnerable he was to the intentions of others or the coarse and automatic systems of war. There was a formula, *infiltrating enemy lines*, that might fall and crush him.

And then the revelation, one she had almost guessed. He had been in the zeppelin that was shot down over the marshlands and had broken in two. He was wounded when one of the girders crushed his ribs, and had been carried from the wreckage and set down at some distance, beneath a tree. When the others were taken prisoner, he was left behind. Just him. Of eighteen crew he was the only one left behind. He still did not understand.

And how did he survive?

Someone came with a cart, loaded him, and brought him to a barn for two nights, then to the olive grove. He did not know why. Twice an old woman arrived to give him a boiled egg and water. Then she didn't come again. He waited and waited. He was thirsty. He was in pain. He thought he was gone. Until that man.

'Stanley,' she offered.

Until Stanley found him. Nothing more, he said. Nothing of war interest.

'The zeppelin?' This was the topic she'd hoped for.

It had been his dream. But on only his second flight, they had crashed. His dream, he repeated.

'Maybach HS engine,' said Olive, wanting to assert a connection.

Jakob's eyes went shiny. He swelled with a feeling that she could not identify. Pride again, perhaps, or sadness, or engineering knowledge.

'Ja, Maybach HS.'

She saw the dream of a boy to float suspended beneath a gigantic balloon, to rise above hubbub and ordinary throng, to leave small busybody faces, the demands of parents, the trivial considerations of school life and good behaviour, for expanse and heaven and tilting horizons. From above, the earth would look sleek and glorious, reconfigured in colour fields and intersecting shapes. She saw the little boy peering down, marvelling in gusty air at the sun travelling along a silver river, and the slanted fields hemmed in by cypress and hedgerow. A road becoming a line, a tiny traveller on a horse. It was Europe she saw, and the land was cultivated, lush.

Grace coughed to remind them both of her official presence.

Armistice. It was a kind of armistice, a commonplace mercy and rest that allowed each an encounter without violence. Olive was struck by how mundane Jakob's conversation had been, devoid of dissembling, or pleading, or boastfulness.

In English Grace declared, 'This man is a survivor of a zeppelin crash over the marshlands. His fellow soldiers were all taken prisoner. He was left behind. He seems to know nothing and in his current condition poses no threat.'

Matron looked disappointed. 'Nevertheless.'

Jakob from Trier changed position, lifting slightly, as if in response to Matron's tone. He winced with pain, and all saw him buckle. He looked directly at Olive, as if to seek approval and to ask, 'Did I do well?'

Now she saw that he had beautiful hooded brown eyes. And she was afraid for him, being so young and ingenuous. Had they been alone, she would have reached out and touched his cheek.

Later, Grace stood beside her and said softly, 'Did you believe him? The zeppelin story and somehow surviving like that?'

And without hesitation Olive said, 'Yes, I believed him.'

FOR ALL SHE had seen in France, the multitudes of wounded, the gaseous light drifting over from the Front, the men breathless at the end, deflating and desperately sucking in life, Grace only now knew herself to be their kin. She felt she was suffocating and in between. With no location for Gerald's body, every place fitted as a possibility. One needed a hole in the ground and a scrawled name planted in the earth beside it.

Later she discovered that grief persists as a perpetual, absent-minded pang. But for now it was in her lungs, which were pinched and incapable. It was deep inside. She noted her symptoms surgically—diffuse pain, palpitation, breathlessness—but there was no physical cause. These were hysterical symptoms. She might have become a 'case', a baggage of ingenious, infuriating links, needing a narrative explanation. In this reflection there was only engulfing sadness. Mourning became her.

As she watched the young German man tell his story to Olive, she felt strangely jealous. To lean above a man's face and hear him talk with infatuated excitement, to be included in rescue and acclamation. He did not know that she was the one who'd actually saved him, that she was the surgeon who had laboured to fix his ribs and sew him back together. That it was she who wound the bandage, made him neat and whole.

The German man had gazed at Olive's face with something like love.

A zeppelin; it made no sense. She'd heard of no zeppelins on the Eastern Front. This was a conspiracy of fantasies. Olive had spoken in the past of zeppelins and their peculiar, deadly enchantment. She told of witnessing an attack in London, and how mesmerised they had been, following a bombing raid in a taxi, watching the bursts of conflagration along Shaftesbury Avenue and beyond. It was an appalling story and she thought Olive shameless for telling it.

And there they were, Olive and the German, speaking of Dresden and Trier, pretending there was no war and no bodies lost, when somewhere on a ridge or in a crater, somewhere in the entire nation of Belgium, her brother had fallen.

Imprecision had made a scandal of her feelings. To know nothing for certain, but to be left with this nation of somewhere and its invasive imaginings.

In another life, Grace had visited Trier with Gerald when they made a short trip to Germany together. It was 1910. She was still studying medicine at Newcastle, but at the end of the year, at Christmas time, had taken a holiday with her brother. Trier was his idea. Like many young men he was obsessed with ancient ruins, and wanted to see the Porta Nigra, a Roman city gate from the first century. Trier once had four gates, he told her, and this was the last one standing. It was a huge sandstone monument, all arched windows and columns, with a hefty tower rising high on one side. In the tower the monk Simeon once lived sequestered as a hermit, tormented by demons. He died demon-bothered and became a saint. The tower was his tomb. For a small fee you could climb the stone steps and enter Simeon's freezing chamber.

They hired a cabriolet and dutifully visited the local ruins of baths and an amphitheatre, and they read descriptions from a tour pamphlet, translating together. They often giggled and mispronounced. Gerald was, he said, deliriously happy. He pulled his lips back, as a child might, to produce a clownish smile for her amusement. At an old inn they drank schnapps and ate tasty fat sausages. It snowed for the entire visit.

This is what she recalled now: how they had stood at the train station and rubbed each other's hands like lovers, how there had been snowdrift over the cinders and piled along the tracks. How they had waited and waited for a train untypically delayed. The body of a frozen pigeon lay near a sign on the platform. With his foot Gerald pushed the dead pigeon beneath a seat, so they would not have to look at it.

Grace had slept very little. She felt almost maddened with tiredness and all the events of the night hours. There was an early morning bustle of unloading and recording provisions: stocking the medicines had kept her busy, and her wandering thoughts were censored by work. Now the hospital was calm and had returned to routine. The air was soft and clear, and it would be another hot day, but evening cool still hung lightly in tucked shady spaces. Recalling Gerald in Trier had opened her stifled lungs. In her fatigue she noted in passing that mind-travel allowed her to breathe more freely.

She must wait a few more hours before she had leave to rest, but there was time at least for a quiet cigarette.

Grace fumbled in her pockets but could find only matches. She might have howled. A Serb convalescent— she had not learned their names—walked by with an armful of firewood and saw her shaking her matches. He unloaded his wood, squatted beside her, and extracted a cigarette from his shirt pocket. Said nothing at all, simply handed it over, gathered up the wood and left. Grace held herself together for the time it took to thank and send him on his way. And for the time it took to smoke his vile-tasting cigarette, which was a poor soldier's cigarette, and not one from her French cache, not one bought from the tobacconist in Salonika that no longer existed.

Now her lungs were all smoke and war. Now she inhaled the entire era and its concealed and unconcealed dangers. The Serb passed by again with another modest load of firewood. He raised a single eyebrow in the merest of greetings. A shy man, a gentleman, leaving her alone. She saw that his weathered face had a yellowish tinge. Vaguely, she recalled he was one of the recovering malarials.

STELLA HAD PULLED through the night and what might have been the crisis of her fever. But the sight of the German man beside her continued to rankle. When Matron arrived she was relieved, thinking the situation would now be resolved, but the soldier remained. Matron didn't move him into the hospital tent with his enemies. She stood henlike and puffed with her hands clasped on her belly, her feet pointing to the corners of the tent, her indignation summoned.

Still a secret, Stella realised; still a problem for them all to contend with. The German was the centre of their attention and a provocative affront; he should never have been brought to the Scottish Women's Hospital. Had she felt well enough she would have said her piece, but Stella could barely string two words together. She guessed that malaria had entered her brain; minuscule blood cells in grey crannies were filling with parasites. The thought terrified her more than the pain spreading in her diaphragm and beginning to inhibit her breathing.

When Olive arrived Stella thought: *You took your time.* She wanted to rebuke her but in Matron's stern presence remained silent. In any case, Olive looked guilty and self-conscious, clearly aware of her transgression in helping the German soldier. There was a moment in

which all in the tent paused and looked at each other—
Olive had said it was not her job to interrogate—and Stella
foresaw the collapse of the matron's authority. Absurdly,
she was reminded of the earthquake in San Francisco,
when she had convinced herself there was a body behind
a wall, and there was none. That had been a wider fear,
she understood now, of what lay hidden, and of her worry
about a world in which a whole city might crumble or
burn. In such a world a woman alone had no guarantee of
safety; no one knew her or saw her individual importance.
Even then she realised it was herself, not the slain or the
injured, that concerned her. She had climbed over bricks
to see, then had to manage her own incredulity.

They talked unhurried, Olive and the German, about
something in common. That much she could see. There
was a genial tone and Olive leant her face close so that
they could speak without raising their voices. Stella
heard a muffled burble of German language moving
in short lines between them, knitting what might have
been collusion and treachery. At the end of the talk
Grace announced that the man had survived a zeppelin
crash and Stella knew at once that this was a fiction,
one certainly invented by Olive. The disappointment was
acute, to know her friend had concocted a story to protect

the enemy. Mistrustful now, she felt Olive had failed a kind of test, one that made her more secluded in her illness and more thoroughly alone.

Before she knew it, the group had dispersed, and Stella was left in the staff tent with the other malarials and the odious soldier, sleeping now with painkillers and unaware of the magnitude of his nuisance.

Someone came into the tent to remove their waste. Stella heard the slosh, smelt the tang, was newly downcast. Then the basins and buckets returned, cleaned, and the cycle began again. She had formulated it: apart from physical symptoms, illness was the combination of repetition, boredom and unwanted memory. It was a shabby formula, but fitted, and she was again impatient to recover.

Edith was a regular in the staff tent and, like Stella, needed an enemy. She thought it disgraceful that they were treating a German soldier. As she busied herself with linen, folding, smoothing and stacking, she confided that she always did what she was told, but in this case was near mutiny and knew they were in the wrong.

'And with our own malarials!' she said, as if location in the hospital was the worst of the soldier's sins. Her frizzy head bobbed and flared in anger at what she had to endure.

Stella saw in Edith an admirable spirit of rebellion, and indicated she too thought their Empire spirit was mocked by the German's presence. Her mind swam with slogans and simple rhymes. Had she not been sealed in her illness, she would have offered a speech on the loyalty of Outlanders to Homelanders, the honour of the Scotsky *sestres* and the duty to prevail.

'Our boys!' Edith went on, with no need to construct a sentence. It was enough to name her side and give voice to her patriotism.

Stella became confused as the day wore on. When she was awake, she checked that she had not been murdered by the German; when asleep she dreamt fever-dreams that were a mesh of violence and turmoil. At times it was a stupor, a long sullen unknowing, in which faces came and went and her sense of the real was sporadic. She heard the German man mutter something and hoped he was suffering. Then she was inside again, relapsed into her insect-invaded brain.

And at some stage Stella looked up and saw a zeppelin. It floated into their tent and thrummed above them with *brrrr* and malignant intent. She expected bombs to fall or men to leap on her from above. It was a fearsome, foreign body, bulging monstrously close. Shivers and more shivers. Her chills came from the airship and zapped like lightning bolts into her body. Icy lightning, fright, the whimper her voice had become.

When the fever subsided, she was in ordinary discomfort, but knew herself safe. The zeppelin disappeared and her reasoning partially returned. This was how it would be for now, the fluctuation of reason and delusion, each ambushed by infirmity.

She recalled Olive's betrayal and was again dismayed. She had never felt so lonely and so far from home.

RABBIT STEW FOR lunch. Stanley scoffed a spoonful from a steaming tin and prepared his mules. At the trenches the others had been given a tot of rum, so he knew that the fighting must be serious. There had been a dawn bombardment, they said, and now there was irregular shelling, building to a bigger assault. From where he waited with the mules he could hear the thud and rumble of their own artillery, taking position. The war was back in his head: he pulled at his mules and prepared them for the inevitable wounded; he moved through his drills, his instructions and his own rituals of preparedness. He quoted Donne to himself, *What if this present were the world's last night?* so that he could keep in view what his father called the perspective of eternity. He touched his chest where his heart was, he touched his forehead and his ears. He listed his Holy Rhymers, including, for luck, Botticello.

And, oh yes, he was lily-livered and God-fearing and weird; and in the proper shemozzle of their misadventure he was but one small and bespectacled man, mule-wallah, raver, bloody good drawer, who looked to be worth nothing as he came from the trembly woods with his mules and assembled them and ran into fire with the stretchers, then back before the clout of detonation and dirt rising up in a wall and falling over them like a tarpaulin blocking the sun; and though bandy at the knees, he was fast and he knew how to tie a travoy, and when others were blown to buggery he ran in, mad in the face of recoil and discharge, dodging gunfire from the north-west and from the north-east, and seeing the two o'clock target of the Lewis gunner knew they were for it, and all the ranks that he saw, private and sergeant and lance corporal and lieutenant and captain, and all like him, all alike, everyone barmy and afraid.

The sapper who helped him was Irish: Joe, he was called, Joe, a short man like himself but strong and good with the mules. Blue eyes, a sharp nose. It almost broke Stanley's heart when they loaded George onto the stretcher, but a quick appraisal said leg wound and survival so he could face him and say, 'Blighty,' as if it was a joke between them, and then push on to the dressing station and a breather and lie doggo for just a minute and see, yes, all of it fickle, and lucky or luckless unevenly distributed. 'Who would perish,' his father once said, 'while the sun is shining?' And it came to him, this sentence and the face waiting for the healing shadow, his father and his mother too, and swimming in the Odney weir with Harold. Ah, a swim, such joy for the doubting and formless spirit; and

Joe said Saint Barbara herself, patron saint of gunners and blasters, had no better charm for it than sunshine and water. Joe spat into a tin pot and extracted from somewhere two Mackintosh toffees and they had one each, tooth-rot hard, what a mouthful, and left tiny paper twists twinkling in the mucky earth behind them.

The faces of the mules were baleful and patient, and they were tired of this gradient and the lugging and the whole back and forth. But still he whispered in their mule ears and loved them each one, but especially Star who answered him in Spanish and was his own world apart. You would think it futile, Stanley said later, seeing George's blood-sodden puttee, or worse a gobbet on wire or spattered khaki that was a man, but from above he saw the round Tommy helmets in the trench side by side like small bronze cupolas, sheltering each head, and with his mouth still toffee-sweet, and plucky Joe pulling the mules firm and guiding by pressing at their heads, decided he would live.

THE PRISONERS TAKEN after the crash of the zeppelin confirmed his existence: he was Jakob Zussman, from Trier, and one of their crew.

Late afternoon now and Olive was cleaning her engine, flushing dirt from the radiator, wiping gaskets and cylinders, when Matron came to tell her that the German must be united with other prisoners of war at the camp near Salonika. Time and resources had been wasted because she had been waylaid by a Tommy. It was an army job, not theirs. It had been foolish to stop for a random appeal—goodness only knows what he was doing there—when she had the provisions to protect and a task of her own to perform.

Matron said 'demarcation of responsibilities' and Olive heard in her phrase yet another border erected and fought over.

It was that time of the day, just before sunset, when mosquitoes were about. Some of the nurses wore masks at their faces and long hot gloves. They were dispensing quinine and pulling mosquito nets above the men in their care, and moved quietly with their veils and their trains of gauze, stepping between the stretchers soft as brides walking to an altar, soft as tiptoeing spies. The men were compliant and thanked the sisters for their attention.

This was the community of the hospital. With no wind and half-light and this winding down after daytime, it was possible to eavesdrop on conversations and to hear the tinkle of syringes in a pan. Some of the men had been given cigarettes, so that low-down smoke began its threading and gentle dispersal, and Olive craved one for herself. She sat on an upturned bucket at the entrance to the tent, squinted into the distance, lit up and inhaled. She felt herself slacken when she knew she must stay upright: so much still to do; so much still to hold together.

The sky was salmon pink, so that now the heat seemed fiery. There was a clatter of dinner preparations and a distant rumble of Krupp guns. She wanted to sit, just sit, with a second cigarette, but decided to return to the staff sick tent. She must talk to Stella; she must give a cigarette to Jakob and tell him he would be rejoining his crew.

Stella was awake and scornful. Her face was aflame. She said to Olive, 'You took your time,' repeating her earlier whinge. It was a hostile greeting. Stella was incoherent in her speech, so they talked of nothing in particular as Jakob looked on with interest. Olive felt her compassion tested, that Stella should be so tough, speaking of Jakob only as an enemy, refusing fellow feeling, accusing her of lying and going soft. She was afraid of zeppelins, she said. 'The one you brought here with you.'

Olive was confused; Stella had seen an imagined airship and held her responsible.

Stella was in pain and demoralised. She was pitiable, Olive told herself. Remember this.

Jakob beckoned, so she joined him, saying to Stella: 'Back in a moment.'

Olive lit a cigarette, sucked it bright, and placed it in Jakob's mouth. He gave a shy glance: *'Danke.'* Looked away, inhaled greedily. The cigarette stayed stuck at his bottom lip until he removed it himself, lifting his right hand slowly, wanting to make the treat last.

'How do you feel?' she asked.

And he took another puff and said, *'Nie besser!'* And smiled at her, his lips parting, his expression open and affectionate.

There was a tall man standing at the tent entrance with Edith. A patient, evidently; he had a bandage across his head and was shaky on his feet. Olive saw him sway, then straighten, like one ordered to attention. The impression was of someone lost, delirious, who had wandered into the wrong tent.

'There,' said Edith, pointing in their direction.

The tall man lifted his army revolver and aimed. There was no time to duck. Jakob was hit in the throat, and his head yanked back and shuddered. A splatter of blood, a gush. A retching rough cough. Instinctively, Olive put her hands to his wound; then a second shot went searing through her left forearm.

The man stumbled forward, maundering, still holding his revolver ahead of him. He shot twice again and Jakob shook with the force of his own death.

Olive will remember the blood copious, splashing and streaming. The stillness of the shooter and the agitation around him. There was no saving Jakob but she kept her hands at his throat, not thinking this might somehow save or revive him, but because her mind was halt and disbelieving. Not thinking at all.

Someone from behind grabbed the tall man and he did not resist. He dropped his revolver, turned and was tugged away. Edith had fallen to the floor and Grace had rushed in. And Olive held his neck still, but it was all substance now, slippery pulp and surprisingly warm, no Jakob there but the waste of him, the waste of a man, of Jakob Zussman from Trier, who had been lately smoking a cigarette, smiling and talking and fully alive. She glanced at his face, which appeared surprised. And then she saw her own bleeding and felt her own slash of pain. Her arm had opened and it too was now streaming blood, so that when she looked down at her lap it might have been a red pool she looked into.

CLOSER, GRACE SAW that his frown was now permanent. His head was back and the mess was mighty. She had to coax Olive to remove her hands from his throat. She held a cloth firm to Olive's wound and called for help.

The merciless drive of the last few days had arrived at this, a man shot in a hospital. Her own faint contempt had been a kind of complicity, complaining of his presence, wanting him gone. All she believed in was now asunder. To kill a man in hospital, a man she had tended. It was atrocity no less than that of men in battle.

Edith had begun screaming, so someone led her away. Then a dense quiet fell, the other patients looking on. Olive sat on the floor, staring at her bloodied skirt. Two orderlies lifted Olive by the elbows to move her to the surgery tent. She staggered between them and did not look back.

Grace prepared herself for what she judged was a straightforward operation.

Washed her hands, wringing them, washed once again.

Afterwards, when the others in her tent were asleep, she sat on her stretcher with a single lit candle on a plate. The candlelight sputtered, unstable. She listened to the wind and wondered if it would rise in the night. She cupped her hand around the flame and read again the letter from her brother.

Repetition for emphasis.

Grace was struck by the life restored in his words. His voice was still there. His undeluded, wry questioning and his implicit love. The grasp of small detail that made him real at a distance. Badminton at Craiglockhart. Sleeping on the grass in full sunshine. The reddened eyes of fellow patients, who had suffered electricity, or worse.

Again, she felt it as a suffocation. The pain of his death lodged in her chest and her lungs were brackets around a void.

Olive had been sewn as she had sewn the German; and they were stitched together, all of them, in coagulate association. Grace had touched their interior.

Her mind was tumbling. She and Gerald had once read Shakespeare together. It had been a summer replete with birdsong and reading, radiant with pre-war complacency and ease. The rosy breast of a robin, calling unseen. The red sky at night, shepherd's delight. Her sleeve stained with an oval blot of strawberry jam. Gerald was sitting on a cushion, vividly alive, a volume open on his lap. He was explaining with an ironic grin the ancient word 'incarnadine'.

Grace would take a bromide to help her sleep. She would medicate herself in the hope that the right words would become things. She would blow out the candle and trust in the dark.

IT WAS A kind of ruffle in time. Stella was not sure what pleat she'd slipped into, but all that occurred was compressed and incredibly fast. Olive had been by her side and next thing she was holding the throat of the German as he bled great rivers. Then Olive was bleeding too and all Stella saw was disaster, thinking that in some way she might have caused this red, or that the zeppelin had caused this red, or that together they had fallen into another kind of war. Her head ached and she wanted to call out but could not; silently she watched as Grace arrived and Olive was taken away, and then two Serbian soldiers lifted the body of the German. Others were gathering up the bloody sheets and mopping the duckboards with pink-headed mops and expunging all the signs of what had happened, or had not.

Someone not Edith arrived to give her a night sedation and she took it, as the others did, because, because. Because she wanted to leave. Because she could not stay in a tent that had been the scene of such bloodletting.

Before she sank away, she thought of her lost hat with the Parma violets.

She thought that she might owe Olive an apology, that their friendship mattered to her in a way she couldn't express, and that the wrong word became the wrong thing and wrecked everything, like war.

WHEN STANLEY CHECKED his kit bag late at night, his folio of drawings was missing. Misplaced, or stolen, or blown away in the wind. Apart from the portraits he'd freely given to his subjects, he would have no record but memory of his time in Macedonia. And his memory was jumbled and not clearly drawn lines. His memory was shot.

Humans, said his father, do not have *tapetum lucidum*.

Stanley sat like a petulant child with his legs drawn up and his chin on his knees. His mind churned with the images of the long, difficult day, but nothing resolved in clarity or made any meaning. Forsaken, private, he managed a little sob. He rolled his gaze to the heavens and like a sozzled old geezer began to hum. It took a minute to realise he hummed the hymn his father had sung, the sonorous Bach hymn he knew the words of, but not the sense.

Ah, the church, and the garden which was made and remade.

He thought of the man he found half dead in the olive grove. Such beautiful brown eyes. The weight of lifting him.

He wondered how the man was recovering and what would happen to him now.

OLIVE FOUND HERSELF in the staff tent on a stretcher beside Stella. So she was still here, where it all happened. Stella was loudly snoring and the tent was beginning to tremble with rising wind.

She tried not to think of the humid, oozy blood of Jakob Zussman, dying.

She thought of her father, ambling in the green shade of his ferns. Of her sister. Her niece. But they were fleeting as cinema.

People said 'after the war', but they also said 'for the duration', as if war had no schedule and would go on forever.

It was intolerable: 'for the duration'.

The burnt city. That was the omen. That was the sign everything was coming apart. Demolition by fire.

The bromide was beginning to work. The pain receded. She began her German grammar, whispering, to keep herself safe.

AUTHOR'S NOTE

This novel centres on four characters, two Australian and two British, who volunteered for medical service in the First World War. Three are women connected with the Scottish Women's Hospital, a group of field hospitals established by suffragettes in Scotland in 1914. Their staff were wholly women and mostly volunteers, and by the end of the war they ran fourteen hospitals, serving in Corsica, France, Malta, Romania, Russia, Macedonia and Serbia. The fourth figure, a man, was a medical volunteer with the Royal Berkshires Infantry.

These characters were inspired by and are loosely based on actual historical figures who worked in the vicinity of the city of Salonika, now Thessaloniki, in 1916–1917. Olive King, daughter of a prominent Sydney banker, was an ambulance driver, wealthy enough to supply her own ambulance and provisions. She later joined the Serbian army. Stella Miles Franklin volunteered as an orderly and was assigned an assistant cook/orderly role. She left within six months but wrote an account of her time in the hospital and went on to become a leading Australian writer. Grace Pailthorpe was a British surgeon, raised as a Plymouth Brethren, who became a Freudian psychoanalyst and a surrealist painter. Stanley Spencer was one of Britain's most famous painters of the twentieth century. After his war service he painted scenes from memory of his year or so in Macedonia, at the Eastern Front.

All four historical figures succumbed to serious bouts of malaria and were returned ill to England, where they had enlisted.

There is nothing I've discovered in the historical record that confirms these figures met or knew each other: this is a work of fiction, not history. For this reason, and others, no character has a surname.

Salonika was the second great Ottoman city (after Constantinople) and the chief army port supplying the Eastern Front in the First World War. It was largely destroyed in the Great Fire of Salonika in August 1917. I have tried to honour historical fact but also made some changes for narrative ends. The downing of a zeppelin near Salonika occurred in May 1916, not in August 1917. The 'skeleton' of the zeppelin was displayed as a war trophy in front of Salonika's famous White Tower. The family circumstances for each character are a mixture of biographical fact and fiction.

'Taking liberty' might be one definition of the imaginative excursions of fiction. This is a novel which takes many liberties and is not intended to be read as a history.

ACKNOWLEDGMENTS

This novel was written in circumstances of unusual isolation, during which time I was away from my home. I am enormously grateful for the moral support offered, mostly by email.

Special thanks to Kyra Giorgi and Victoria Burrows for reading so assiduously the first version of this text, and to Mireille Juchau, Susan Midalia and Marion M. Campbell, without whose dear support this project could not have been completed. Thanks to Jane Novak and to Michael Heyward and the team at Text Publishing, ever patient and professional; and to Alaina Gougoulis, whose editorial advice was exceptionally wise and clever. Thanks too to David Malouf for permission to quote his poem and for his companionable interest in the city of Salonika. I would also like to acknowledge the Australia Council for the Arts for their generous, flexible and compassionate support of this project, and for their ongoing commitment to arts practice and practitioners in Australia.

To Peter and Kevin, my brothers, this novel is dedicated to the memory of our mother.

The following resources have been invaluable in prompting my own imaginings:

J. S. Bach, *Als Jesu Christus in der Nacht*, lyrics by Johann Heermann, BWV 265

Pat Barker, *The Regeneration Trilogy* (Penguin, 1991, 1993, 1995)

Herbert Corey, 'On the Monastir Road', *National Geographic*, Vol. 31, no. 5 (May 1917): 383–412

Thomas Dilworth, *David Jones: Engraver, soldier, painter, poet* (Vintage, 2017)

S. Miles Franklin, 'Nemari Ništa (It Matters Nothing): Six months with the Serbs', in Slobodanka Vladiv-Glover (ed.), *Transcultural Studies: A series in interdisciplinary research*, Special Issue Vol. 10, no. 2 (January 2014): 1–21

Ariela Freedman, 'Zeppelin Fictions and the British Home Front', *Journal of Modern Literature*, Vol. 27, no. 3 (Winter 2004): 47–62

David Jones, *In Parenthesis* (Faber and Faber, 1937/1978)

Hazel King (ed.), *One Woman at War: Letters of Olive King 1915–1920* (Melbourne University Press, 1986)

Fiona MacCarthy, *Stanley Spencer: An English vision* (Yale University Press, 1997)

Mark Mazower, *Salonica, City of Ghosts: Christians, Muslims, and Jews* (HarperCollins, 2004)

Lee Ann Montanaro, 'Surrealism and Psychoanalysis in the

Work of Grace Pailthorpe and Reuben Mednikoff: 1935–1940', unpublished PhD thesis, University of Edinburgh, 2010

Alan Palmer, *The Gardeners of Salonika: The Macedonian campaign 1915–1918* (Faber and Faber, 2011)

Jill Roe, *Stella Miles Franklin: A biography* (HarperCollins, 2010)

Scottish Women's Hospital Archive: https://archiveshub.jisc.ac.uk/search/archives/292e5ea5-6a7c-3c1d-8034-db2af7c32be5

Andrekos Varnava, 'The Vagaries and Value of the Army Transport Mule in the British Army during the First World War', *Historical Research*, Vol. 90, no. 248 (May 2017): 422–446

The sound of zeppelins is derived from Katherine Mansfield. C. K. Stead (ed.), *The Letters and Journals of Katherine Mansfield: A selection* (Allen Lane, 1977): 56

A scene in this novel derives from a letter from 1915 in which Virginia Woolf congratulates her friend Lady Eleanor Cecil: 'I rejoiced to hear of you following Zeppelin in a taxi; such it is to have the blue blood of England in one's veins: my literary friends hide in cellars, and never walk at night without looking at the sky.' Nigel Nicolson (ed.), *Virginia Woolf: The Question of Things Happening: Letters 1912–1922* (Hogarth Press, 1976): 64 (cited in Ariela Freedman)